New to the Game 2

Lock Down Publications and Ca$h
Presents
New to the Game 2

A Novel by *Malik D. Rice*

Lock Down Publications
P.O. Box 944
Stockbridge, Ga 30281

Lock Down Publications
Like our page on Facebook: Lock Down Publications @
www.facebook.com/lockdownpublications.ldp
Cover design and layout by: **Dynasty Cover Me**
Book interior design by: **Shawn Walker**
Edited by: **Lashonda Johnson**

Malik D. Rice

Stay Connected with Us!

Text **LOCKDOWN** to 22828 to stay up-to-date with new releases, sneak peaks, contests and more…

Thank you!

Submission Guideline.

Submit the first three chapters of your completed manuscript to ldpsubmissions@gmail.com, subject line: Your book's title. The manuscript must be in a .doc file and sent as an attachment. Document should be in Times New Roman, double spaced and in size 12 font. Also, provide your synopsis and full contact information. If sending multiple submissions, they must each be in a separate email.

Have a story but no way to send it electronically? You can still submit to LDP/Ca$h Presents. Send in the first three chapters, written or typed, of your completed manuscript to:

LDP: Submissions Dept
P.O. Box 944
Stockbridge, Ga 30281

DO NOT send original manuscript. Must be a duplicate.

Provide your synopsis and a cover letter containing your full contact information.

Thanks for considering LDP and Ca$h Presents.

Malik D. Rice

CHAPTER 1

It was a cold, rainy day in the streets of East Atlanta. There weren't many people outside in the nasty weather but there was always somebody that would be out-and-about no matter what kind of weather was displayed on the forecast. People were walking in-and-out of the Target store in the plaza on the Northern end of Moreland Avenue.

"Whose bright idea was it to do this shit in front of a store on the hottest street in East Atlanta?" asked Quay.

Toe-Tag sighed deeply. "Vonte," he answered dryly. He hadn't been his usual talkative self during the past few days.

"This shit don't make no sense," said Quay.

Monster pulled his hood over his head after securing the black bandana around his face. "He said he wants it to be messy, and he wants it to be done in a public place."

"I knew that nigga was trying to get us out the picture. He don't like us," said Quay.

Toe-Tag shook his head. "He just don't like me."

"For whatever reason. Why he want, Kandice's head anyway?" said Quay.

Toe-Tag looked at Quay through slanted eyes and spoke through a mean mug. "Nigga, you sure do got a lot of questions to ask today. I don't know why he wants shawty dead and I don't care. All I know is that Vonte is our Underboss and we take orders from him."

Quay nodded in understanding. "You right, but her daddy is the fuckin' Pope. I'm not trying to get fucked up behind this shit."

"We can't, if anybody gets fucked up behind the shit, it'll be Vonte." A slow smile appeared on Toe-Tag's face at the thought. "Now that I think about it. I might have a way to get my soul back from his ass."

A long ten minutes later, Kandice walked out of Target with her female friend. Kandice was pushing a cart half-filled with grocery bags while her tall, red-headed friend held a big Burberry umbrella over both of their heads.

"How you want it done lil' bro'?" Monster asked while looking at Toe-Tag.

Toe-Tag looked out the tinted window of the Nissan minivan that they sat in and shook his head. He'd known Kandice most of his life. They went to school together and knew a lot of the same people. Shit, she was friends with Shanay. She was a good girl, and he really didn't want to see anything happen to her, but it had to be her time because he didn't have a choice. She had to go. "Two to the head."

Toe-Tag lit the cigarette that had been hanging in his mouth for the past few minutes and leaned back in his seat while Quay and Monster hopped out to go handle the business. He was the brains, and it was time for him to fall back which meant he had to stay out of the field. As a made man, he wasn't even supposed to be on the scene, but he had to at least oversee the mission. He already felt bad for not participating.

Monster let Quay lead the mission. He was trying to move up in the chain-of-command and needed to put in as much work as possible. Monster was just there to back him up just in case.

The sun was descending and the dark clouds that hovered under it blocked most of its shine. It was 4:00 p.m., but if someone had just awakened from a slumber, they would swear it was nighttime. They stalked through the cars in the parking lot stealthy in a crouch. Their guns were drawn, and they both had their game faces on even though they couldn't be seen under the bandanas.

Quay made a rapid stop and Monster almost bumped into him. "What the fuck you doing?" he asked curiously.

"Shut up, nigga, I got this. They walking up now. I'm about to handle the business real quick, and smooth. Watch how it's done."

Kandice and her friend speed-walked right past them. They were busy talking about a mixtape release party that they planned on attending later that night, but little did they know, they would never make it.

Quay popped up from behind the car and came up with his Glock 23 pointed at Kandice's back. He put one in her back and sent her straight to the ground crying out in pain. She looked like a pretty mermaid rolling around in the parking lot puddle. Her friend dropped the umbrella and took off running while screaming frantically for help.

Quay looked at her and shook his head. Usually, he would've picked her off so she couldn't get away, but she wasn't the target so he could care less about it. Other civilians were running for cover and speeding off in their cars. This was the part of East Atlanta where a lot of white people hung out at, so that meant plenty of police around to protect them. He knew they were probably already on the way.

"Pleassseee! Don't killl mee-eeee!" she cried out desperately with a hand in front of her like it was going to stop another bullet. "I'm—I'm p-pr-pr—"

"You what! Bitch hurry up and spit it out! I ain't got all night!" he commanded urgently. He'd already wasted too much time, but something told him he needed to hear what she had to say.

She spit up a healthy glob of blood. "I'm preggg—nant!" she informed in pain. It sounded like she was losing breath.

He closed his eyes for half of a second and took a much-needed deep breath before taking two steps closer to her. He looked down at her pleading eyes. She was so pretty, and innocent, but she had to go. He pulled the trigger twice inviting the two hallow tipped bullets to their new home in her face.

"What the fuck took you so long nigga? Let me find out you choking on missions and shit!" Monster barked at Quay once they got back in the van.

Dreek swerved through traffic like a pro getting them as far away from the crime scene as possible.

"She was telling me something, man."

"What could the bitch possibly be telling you other than not to kill her?"

Quay slumped down in his seat. "She was pregnant, shawty."

"What!" Toe-Tag asked urgently. "What the fuck you just say, Quay?"

"Man, you heard me, she said she was pregnant."

He couldn't believe it. "You sure you heard her, right?"

"I know what I heard."

Toe-Tag looked off into space trying to put all the missing pieces together. If Vonte wanted her dead, and she was pregnant, that could only mean one thing. "That fuck nigga the Devil for real. That was his baby inside, Kandice."

***

Toe-Tag walked into his empty apartment and took a seat on the couch in the living room. He sucked up the darkness and tried to enjoy the quietness. He wanted so bad to talk to God, and ask for forgiveness, but why would He even consider giving a nigga like him the time of day? He took lives for a living and went about it like it was a regular taxpaying job. How could God forgive something like that?

He'd taken eleven lives, and he was only seventeen, with his current made-man stripes, he was a living legend. He was only a few months older than his predecessor, Rampage, so that now made him the youngest made man in Dilluminati. "Bro'. Wassup, my nigga? A nigga missing you already. Shit crazy out here in these streets." He figured he'd be better off talking to his homeboy in hell than talking to the man who ruled over a Holy place he'd never make it into.

"Bodies dropping left-and-right, everybody getting robbed, and all types of shit. Shanay left me, and I let her go because I love her. I ain't gon' do shit but fuck her life up. I been surrounded by all these fake ass niggas and bitches. I don't trust nobody but Monster for real. I'm really mad we had got into it before you left my nigga. We was better than that. But guess what? When I get down there with you, we gon' be better than Shaq and Kobe. I ain't gon' hold you up, though. I know you probably knee-deep in some demon pussy right now. Live it up, my nigga. I love you like the little brother I never had."

It wasn't until after he got finished talking that he noticed a few tears had escaped his eyes. "What the fuck wrong with you, nigga? We don't do no crying," he asked himself then stated while wiping the tears with the sleeve of his sweater. "Sitting right here talking to myself." He chuckled. "I'm fucked up, shawty."

He closed his eyes and prepared to get a little sleep hoping he didn't have a nightmare about one of his murder victims trying to kill him.

***

Quay was in the shower trying to get the image of Kandice's pretty face, and voice, out of his head. *"I'm preggg—nant!"*

He shut his eyes tightly and stepped under the water. In his line of work, you were expected not to have feelings, just instincts. You had to transform into an animal to survive in the concrete jungle he was in. The older he got, the more work he put in. The more work he put in, the more of his soul was lost to him.

His new girl, Diamond walked into the bathroom. She was a cute, dark-skinned stripper that he'd been dealing with for the last month. He wanted to make her a Dinero Girl, but her whole family was Crip, so she couldn't do it. Her big brother was an O.G. and would surely kill her if she dropped her blue flag for an American flag. They still fucked with each other and made it work as best they could.

"Baby, a nigga named, Handsome, called your phone saying he's on the way to come get you. You literally just walked in this muthafucka. Now you got to leave right back out? Ain't that much work in the world."

He thought about why Handsome would be coming to pick him up and couldn't think of anything. "Something must've just came up because ain't no jobs I know of right now."

"In between me stripping, and you in them streets, ain't no real-time for us to spend time together. I don't know about this shit, Quay."

He cut the water off, grabbed a towel, and stepped out of the shower. "What the hell you trying to say?" he asked while drying his body off in front of her.

She sat on the toilet, moved the silky royal blue weave out of her face, and looked up at him seriously. "How the hell did we even start taking each other serious? We trying to live a fairytale. I'm a stripper, and you a killer. What was we gon' do start a family?"

"I mean—that would've been nice," he answered dully. "So, you leaving?"

12

She blew out a hard breath. "Ughhh! See! That's that shit I'm talking about right there. I just basically broke up with you, and you standing her all nonchalant and shit. I stopped fucking with niggas like you for a reason."

He stepped into a clean pair of Givenchy briefs. "Why?"

"Y'all don't know how to love because y'all don't got no fucking souls," she spat before getting up and walking out of the bathroom.

He didn't try to stop her either.

Malik D. Rice

CHAPTER 2

"This is Ralph Nelson, reporting live from Channel 4 news. I'm here standing in the parking lot in front of a Target on Moreland avenue a couple of feet away from the very spot where a young lady was killed with three bullets. One to the back, and two to the head. She was later identified as, Kandice Cooper. The only child of, Kareem Cooper, also known as, D.G. Kapo. None of Kandice's personal belongings were missing, so authorities believe that the murder had something to do with her father, who is currently under investigation by the federal government for being a local kingpin. Kareem is now wanted for questioning in the death of his daughter—"

"Wooo-shit! I ain't know they was gon' do that girl like that there!" Vonte exclaimed matter-of-factly.

He was in his downtown loft with a Dinero Girl named, Violence. She was a small bundle of thunder. Her light skin and baby face would fool you into thinking she was harmless, which is how she lured in most of her victims.

"You know it was other ways to go about that situation, right?" she asked from the floor while laying half-naked on a big black mink rug. She loved the feeling of the rug so much she'd just made him make love to her right there where she laid.

He looked down at her from the black leather sofa he sat on imported straight from Germany. "Let that bitch have my baby? Got me fucked up."

"You could've put abortion pills in her food or some shit."

"Damn—why the fuck you ain't been say that?" he asked heatedly.

She shrugged her shoulders. "I guess I wanted to see if you was gon' really do some evil ass shit like that."

"I'm the Devil bitch. You know I ain't fucked up about the next muthafuckas life."

"Ssss, and that's what turns me on the most about your lil' sexy ass."

He shook his head at her. She was just as crazy as him which is probably why they got along so well. He hated to admit it, but she'd probably be the one who he ended up with. She was the only one who could really handle him. "Go make daddy something to eat."

He watched as her tattooed ass jiggled in the leopard printed panties she wore as she walked toward the kitchen, then focused back on the news playing on the TV.

Two reporters were sitting at a table with the city's skyline in their background. "So, Summer, what do you think about the tragedy that took place today? And what do you think about the authorities questioning the father about the death of his own daughter?" Dave, a clean-cut, Caucasian man asked his coworker, a super-tanned blonde milf with fake breasts popping out of her blouse.

"It's a very difficult and delicate issue, to be honest. It's no secret that the government has been at a steady war with Dinero Guys all around the country ever since the arrest of their leader, Dinero. Many have accused the government of harassing them, but the truth is that ever since they'd surfaced about nine months ago, the murder rate has risen in *every* single city that Dilluminati calls home. Wherever there's DG, there's death, and the poor little girl who got gunned down earlier today is an example of what I'm talking about." said Summer.

Dave nodded his head in understanding. "I absolutely agree. Spike Lee described them as a society of organized savages who places themselves way above the law."

"And that's sad because he turns around and makes a movie about them." Summer states matter-a-factly.

"Which comes out next year. You would think the public would bash such an organization instead of glorifying it," said Dave.

"Tells you a lot about the world we live in today. We'll be right back with more details about the murder of, Kandice Cooper and the search for her father after this short break," Summer concluded.

Vonte turned the TV off, put the remote down, and picked up his cup of mixed cough syrup. He knew he didn't have to kill Kandice, but he warned her to get the abortion, and she thought shit was a game because Kapo was her father.

"I told you, bitch. All you had to do was what the fuck I told you. I tried to warn you, but you didn't want to listen, now look at you," Vonte said while looking up at the ceiling with an evil smirk on his face.

He didn't see Violence standing off to the side with a hand on her hip and a weird expression on her face. "Boy, you need help," she informed before walking back into the kitchen.

***

Kapo ran into the kitchen to check on his wife. He was preparing to get in the shower when he heard her screaming hysterically, breaking glass, and furniture. Due to everything going on, he didn't know if someone was trying to break in, so he had his Colt 45 pistol in his hand ready to handle business if needed. He wasn't expecting to see Tanya, blacking out by herself throwing a tantrum.

Her hair and clothes were a mess. She looked just like a woman who'd just recently lost her only child. She was now sitting on the floor with her back to the counter and her face in her hand's crying frantically. "Goddd! Whyyy! Whyyy-y-y-yyy! I want my babbbyyy! I want my babbyyy back! Please, Lord! Pleaseee!"

Out of the twenty years, he'd known his wife he'd never seen her so broken in his life and it was fucking him up. Seeing her like that literally made him weak. Knowing that he was probably the cause of his daughter's death made him weak, but he had to be strong for Tanya. She needed him.

"Baby, it's okay! It's alright." He got down on the glass littered floor with her and tried to comfort her by wrapping her in his arms.

"Get. The. Fuck. Off me nigga!" She pushed off him and started swinging on him channeling all of her anger onto him. "She's dead because of *you*! It's your fault!" She pushed herself up onto her feet.

"Baby! Stop, don't do this. I need you right now," he cried out to her now on his feet taking steps towards her.

"Don't! Come near me! All this is *your* fault!" She picked up her car key off the counter. "I don't want to see you again, Kareem. I can't live here with you anymore I might kill you in your sleep," she spat before running out of the house with pajamas on and bare feet.

After the pain and shock of what she'd just said wore off a little, he took off after her, but he was too late. She was already speeding up their driveway in her turquoise BMW coupe only to get blocked in by a motorcade of government-issued SUVs.

Kapo sat in a small interrogation room in downtown Atlanta. A bag of Fritos and a pack of cigarettes sat untouched on a rectangular wooden table in front of him. He'd been in the room for the better part of two hours. He looked down at his Hublot watch and sighed deeply. He didn't have the time, or energy to be playing these games with them.

There was a camera in each corner of the ceiling. He stood up, grabbed the chair, walked to the corner by the door and swung the chair at the camera. He did this three times, then returned the chair to its rightful place and sat in it. Three minutes later, three agents entered the room with very unpleasant expressions on their faces.

"Took y'all long enough," Kapo stated while looking up at them with two feet resting on their table.

A tall, muscular, bald man, the biggest agent of the three walked up to him and slapped his feet off the table with so much force that he almost fell out of the chair.

"Have some respect," his deep voice boomed before taking his place standing against the wall directly behind Kapo.

Kapo turned around and looked up at the big guy, then sat right back in his seat and stared the other two agents down.

A very small, pale agent with a big head full of red hair smiled brightly. "Mr. DG Kapo. What an honor to finally meet you. I'm senior special agent, Chinx. This lovely Caribbean lady sitting next to me is, Agent Gill, and that big, handsome fella behind you is, Agent Bridge. I assume you know why you're sitting here today?"

Kapo stared at him blankly. "Where's my lawyer?"

"Well, I'll tell you. You're here because you're a known kingpin in the state of Georgia, and your daughter has just been publicly executed. We have reason to believe that she didn't have any enemies and you brought that horrible fate onto her."

Kapo held his cool. "Call my lawyer."

"Do you not know who I am?"

"Senior special, Agent Chinx. Supervisor of all four investigations that are currently taking place for Dilluminati in Georgia. The supervisor, and participant in the severe beating of two young black men on Bouldercrest road that landed them in the hospital about a month ago. Loving husband and father of two little midget bastard—"

Before he could get the last words out, Agent Bridge caught him with a lethal hook to the side of the face sending him tumbling to the floor in pain.

"Ahhhh-fuck!" he cried out with a hand on his face. He slowly got back up into his seat, adjusted his suit jacket and looked straight at agent Chinx. "He hit like a bitch."

"The instant swelling on the side of your face says different. I see you've done a little homework, which doesn't impress me. Would you like to tell me why your daughter was gunned down like that? We're trying to help you."

"I don't need your help I need my lawyer."

He smiled brightly. "Tanya seems to think she needs our help. As a matter of fact, she's been very helpful to our investigation."

"Fuck you."

The next thing he knew, Agent Bridge's massive arms were wrapped tightly around his neck like a big snake. He grabbed onto the man's arm with both hands gasping for air.

Agent Chinx jumped on top of the table and closed the distance between them. He slapped Kapo with surprising force. "You think you have all the sense, but guess what? You're going down. The whole Dilluminati is on borrowed time."

He reached his hand back and agent Gill placed an iPad in it. "How about you take a look at this."

Agent Bridge let him go and he began coughing gasping for air. When he looked up the iPad was showing Tanya sitting in an identical interrogation room talking to the same agents.

"He never knew all the shit I knew about his dealings in the streets, but he'd be surprised. I got so much dirt on Dilluminati, it's not funny."

New to the Game 2

"Mrs. Cooper, do you think your husband had something to do with the death of your daughter?"

She suppressed a sob. "He didn't have her killed, but I know for a fact she's dead because of him."

"Are you willing to help us bring him down so no one else has to get hurt, including yourself?"

She tried to suppress another sob, but it escaped a little. "Yes." She put her face in her arms and started sobbing uncontrollably screaming Kandice's name.

Agent Chinx moved the iPad out of his face. "You might want to start talking to save yourself. I just want everybody from, Vonte, on up."

Kapo started drawing mucus from his nose, down to his mouth, and spit a nasty glob of spit in agent Chinx's face. The rest was a blur after that, he'd lost consciousness soon after.

Malik D. Rice

CHAPTER 3

There was heavy knocking on Black's front door. He'd sent his baby mother to Western Union to wire his other baby mother some money, and she had a key, so he knew it wasn't her. He wished he'd told her to leave his six-year-old son behind so he wouldn't have to open the door, but little Vernon wasn't there so he had to answer the door himself. It took him a full minute to get completely to his feet from the couch. It felt like his ribs were taking forever to heal.

"Hold the fuck on!" he yelled, then grimaced immediately. He couldn't do anything, besides, think without hurting his ribs.

When he finally made it to the door, he opened it and prepared to curse someone out, but he was caught by surprise. His mother stood there staring at him with tears in her eyes. "You couldn't even bother to show up at your brother's funeral?" she asked accusingly with a voice of someone who'd been crying for days.

"Ma, I just couldn't—"

She held both sides of the door, leaned back, and came forward with her foot extended kicking him in his midsection sending him to the ground in lots of pain.

"Ahhh! What the fuck, ma?" he cried out on the ground balled up in a fetal position.

She kicked him in his side with her powder blue Timberland boot. She was a big woman, so the force from the kick probably broke one of his already fractured ribs. "Fuck nigga, you the reason why he in the dirt. And you got the nerve to miss out on his funeral?" She pulled a pearl 380. out of her purse and pressed the muzzle to his forehead. "Give me one reason why I shouldn't put a bullet in your head right now?"

He looked up at her expectantly. "I'm yo' muthafuckin' son!" he spat painfully.

She pulled the gun back and slapped him across the skull with it. "You ain't shit to me lil' nigga! Stay away from me, and the rest of my muthafuckin' kids." She got up and stormed out of the apartment without closing the door behind her.

Black couldn't do anything but lay there on the floor in pain. He couldn't even get up to close the door to stop the freezing air from rushing into the apartment. "Aggghhh!" he yelled at the top of his lungs.

He'd never felt so helpless in his young life. He just wanted to roll over and die. The pain was unbearable. He just wanted it to stop, inside and out.

***

"What's wrong, Razor? I know you going through a lot, but you, not the only one," Babie said to her newest boyfriend.

He was a sixteen-year-old kid that had just started going to her school. He was from the Westside of Atlanta but changed schools when child protection services took him away from his mother and placed him in a group home, that just-so-happened to be in East Atlanta. "My mamma about to go to prison for the rest of her life and I can't do shit about it. I'm supposed to be out here trying to get her some money for a lawyer."

Babie climbed on top of him and looked down at him. She didn't know what it was about him but judging by the fact that he'd made it into her bed in a short two weeks, there had to be something special about him.

She looked down at his sweet honey eyes and almost melted. "I got some money left over from my brother. Maybe I can help." She'd always been taught to get money from a nigga, never to give, but Razor was different. He was making her do things she never thought she'd do.

He pulled her down for a kiss. "I appreciate that lil' baby, but you and yo' sister need that money. I couldn't take that." She sighed. "I can get Toe-Tag to put you down with his crew. They making crazy money out here. You just gon' have to get your hands dirty because they making blood money."

He looked at her knowingly. "I been Piru my whole life. My mamma Piru. I can't be Dilluminati."

"What them Piru niggas ever did for you? Where they at now, Razor. DG might not have as many numbers as them, but guess what? When you in need they gon' be there. We take care of our own. Your mother might do some jail time, but she won't be in prison forever if we got anything to do with it."

He pushed her off him gently, got out of the bed, and walked over to the window. "I don't even know them niggas, bae," he stated while looking down at a small group of Dinero guys, and girls kicking it in front of an apartment building across from theirs.

She walked up behind him and wrapped her arms around his small torso. "I'm Rampage's little sister. The youngest made man Dilluminati has ever seen. They gon' embrace you on the strength of me. Toe-Tag told me to hit him up if I ever needed something, well this is about to be it."

Razor shook his head. "I don't know about this man."

"Just chill, I got you. You gon' be alright. You built for this shit I can tell."

***

The worst thing about having to depend on one person for anything is that when something happens to that one person, you're shit out of luck. Masio was depending on, Kapo, to keep everything in line, now Kapo was lying unconscious in a hospital bed with his hand cuffed to the rail. Not only was the media having a field day with him, but they were also targeting Dilluminati as a whole. They were using this incident to their advantage.

"Shit would start getting out of hand when I'm in charge. Now I got to clean all this shit up," he was talking to his little brother, Santana on video chat.

Santana was serving time in prison on a murder conviction, that he was fighting to get overturned. He might've been locked up, but he was still living his life. "Just get Freddy to do it."

"Freddy got enough going on. Plus, it's time for me to get up off my ass anyway."

"Who you think whacked Kapo's daughter?"

Masio shrugged his shoulders. "Ain't no telling, I think it was an inside job if you ask me."

Santana gave him a look of pure confusion. "What makes you think that?"

"Georgia got the grimiest camp in America. Shit real cutthroat out here. It's to the point where Dinero guys from other states ain't even trying to come down here. Don't nobody trust us."

Santana shook his head. "Ronte said some shit about being renegade in one of his songs. That's which one we working on?"

"I mean, I guess. I just can't wait until you give that time back and come home. I can't trust nobody but Freddy these days."

"It ain't gon' be what you think big bro'. I'm going to North Carolina with my girl when I get out. If I stay in Georgia I ain't gon' do nothing but come back to prison."

Masio shook his head. "You just gon' abandon all this shit I got set up for you out here? Yo' big brother the Godfather over Georgia! You know what type of pull you gon' have out here?"

"Fuck pull, I just want freedom."

"Whatever. You done let that white girl get in your head. It's all good, though. One day you gon' get tired of living the regular life, you was born for this shit."

"I got to go, man. Keep yo' head up, and don't get whacked out there."

Masio chuckled, knowing he didn't really have to go, but he let it slide. "A'ight lil' nigga." He hung the phone up and looked over at the brown-skinned goddess that laid naked next to him. "What I tell you about listening in on my conversations?"

She rolled her eyes. "I don't have a choice when you talking right in front of me. Plus, I ain't no snitch. You can trust me."

"The only thing I trust is the fact that I know where your whole family lives."

She looked up at him menacingly. "Stop threatening my family!"

"Yeah, Masio, it's not really polite to threaten a lady, you know." 2-Tall chimed in while walking into the big master bedroom with four serious-looking individuals on his heels. They were dressed just as well as he was.

Masio tried to reach for his pistol on the dresser, but a suppressed bullet from one of 2-Tall's guards pushed it off the dresser onto the floor.

"I'm just going to pretend like you didn't just try to reach for your weapon in my presence," said 2-Tall while taking a seat on the small couch on the other side of the room.

27

"Can I leave? I don't got nothing to do with this nigga. We just fucking," the pretty, brown-skin vixen asked, then stated urgently.

"Yes, you can leave. One of my men in the living area will see you out," 2-Tall answered.

Every set of eyes in the room watched her backside as she hurried out of the room in her birthday suit. "Nice piece of ass, but the problem with her type is they're usually for self as you can see," said 2-Tall once she exited the room.

Masio grilled him with a nasty mug and made a mental note to handle the girl if he survived this night. "How the fuck you get in my condo, past my security?"

"Your security is tied up lying face down on the living room floor with gags in their mouths. They're good, but my guys are way better."

Masio tried to get out of bed.

"Ah-ah! I'd rather you stayed in the bed during this little meeting. Won't be too long."

"You could've just set up a meeting like everybody else."

2-Tall leaned back on the couch looking like a super-tall gangster version of NBA star Jimmy Butler in an expensive suit. "I have my reasons for doing everything that I do. You do know why I'm here tonight, don't you?"

"You going up on the prices?"

"For as much of a risk I'm taking by doing business with you, I should, but no. This visit isn't about money, it's about order. Something your camp seems to be severely lacking."

"This camp been like this way before I became the God-father. Don't come up in here like it's my fault these niggas moving like this."

"I know it's not your fault, but guess what? You're the Godfather, and it's your job to clean this shit up. If you don't, I'll find somebody who can. And you know what happens to retired Godfathers, don't you?" He stood up and prepared to leave. "I'll give you a hint, start at the bottom."

***

"You looking at it like you want to count it, or somethin'," Vonte said to Toe-Tag who was in the back of his Bentley with him.

"This ten-thousand, I charge ten a body. Kandice was pregnant. That was another life, so I need another ten," said Toe-Tag while holding the bankroll in the air towards Vonte.

"I'll give you five more, that was half a life."

"Come on with it. Why you have her whacked anyway?"

Vonte looked at him sideways. "In this line of work, questions not allowed. I know you're new to this shit, but you better get with the program quick," he warned after handing Toe-Tag $5,000.

"Fuck it, everybody got their reasons. Anybody else you need whacked?"

Vonte shook his head. "Nah, but I'll let you know if I do."

"Good, because I got my own business to tend to."

"Cool with me as long as I get my cut."

Toe-Tag flicked a middle finger at him before stuffing the money in his coat pocket and getting out of the car.

"What that nigga say about the extra ten?" Monster asked as they watched the Bentley and two Escalades, drive toward the exit of their apartment complex.

"He gave me five, talking about it was half a body."

Monster smiled. "It's always something with that nigga there."

"I'm gon' put a bullet in his head, mark my words."

"Let's go lil' nigga. We got places to be, and people to see," Monster said while patting him on the back before leading the way toward the rented black BMW truck they were currently riding in.

"Toe-Tagggg! Wait!" Babie yelled from about three buildings down. She had some skinny nigga walking with her that couldn't be from around their way because he wasn't dressed in all black.

"Babie, wassup lil' sis, you a'ight?" Toe-Tag asked before looking at Razor menacingly. "Who the fuck is this lil' nigga?"

Babie closed the distance between her and Razor and wrapped an arm around his waist. "This is my boyfriend, Razor."

"I guess. Wassup though? I really got some business I need to handle."

"I need you to stamp him. He trying to get some money to buy his mamma a lawyer. She locked up for killing the nigga that killed his daddy."

Toe-Tag looked from Razor to Babie then Monster. "It's up to you, I done made enough decisions for the day. My head hurt. You gon' be calling the shots for the rest of the day," he informed before walking off to the truck.

Babie looked up at Monster. "I won't ask y'all for nothing else, just put my nigga on."

"You really like this nigga, huh?" he stated while scanning Razor with an amused expression on his face. "I probably can find something for the nigga to do."

"Uh-uh, he ain't gon' be just another shooter out here. I want him on Toe-Tag's kill-team."

Monster laughed. "You must be smoking that shit lil' girl? It's niggas that been putting in crazy work, and still ain't made it on the kill-team yet. How you think they gon' feel if I stamp this nigga, and put him on the kill-team? He gon' have to go through the motions like everybody else."

"I'm asking y'all to do me a favor, Monster. He official, and he about that shit. He'll catch one-hundred bodies if he got to!" she spat matter-a-factly, but she didn't see Razor looking down at her sideways through the dreads that covered most of his face.

"Your man don't look as confident as you sound," he teased.

Razor stuck his chest out. "Looks can be deceiving. You heard my girl, I'm about this shit," he boasted with confidence he didn't have.

The truth was that he was known for shooting at niggas, not actually shooting niggas, let alone, actually killing them. He was in over his head.

Monster flashed a smug smirk. "How about this—if he makes it through one night with me, and Toe-Tag, I'll stamp the lil' nigga and make sure his mamma get a good lawyer personally."

Babie smiled. "Okay!"

"You got a gun lil' nigga?"

Razor had to breathe deeply to stop his heart from beating out of his chest. He wanted to back out of the ordeal so bad but didn't want to look soft in front of Babie, so he just went along with it and pulled a 25 out of his pocket. "Yeah."

Monster laughed heavily. "What the fuck you gon' do with that, shoot a mosquito? I'm gon' get you a real gun. Come on, the night starts right now." He walked off toward the truck.

"You got this, baby," Babie assured before placing a sweet kiss on his lips.

"I hope so," he said before following Monster.

Babie watched her man walk away with pride. She hoped he turned out to be just as great as her brother. Rampage made it hard for other niggas because he fucked her head up into thinking that if a nigga wasn't like him, he wasn't the one for her. So naturally, she'd be trying to mold a nigga into Rampage until she got it right.

CHAPTER 4

"Y'all niggas got us in the middle of y'all bullshit," Turk told Quay while they ate inside McDonald's on Moreland Avenue. They had a few shooters a piece with them sitting at other tables.

"What the hell you talkin' about?" Quay asked with a mouth full of fries.

"That shit y'all got going on with them G-shine niggas. Y'all got us in the middle of y'all shit."

Quay looked at him confusingly. "We ain't beefing. Vonte handled all that shit."

"I know that much, but the hate still in the air. Y'all still don't like each other. So, now we got to choose sides 'cause we can't play both sides."

"What you want me to do?"

"Ain't nothing you can do. I'm just letting you know what we going through trying to stay loyal to y'all niggas. Anyway, you said you got something for me?"

"You ever heard of a nigga named, B-Low, from Cobb County?"

Turk scrunched his face together stretching the tattoos he had on his light-skinned face. "Uhhh—hell nah, don't ring no bells. You need the nigga gone?"

"Nah, not this one. He making some big moves out there and my baby mamma got the drop on his tender dick ass."

"A'ight, what you need me for?"

"I don't need you. I'm just fucking with you how you fuck with me."

Turk smiled. "You always been a solid nigga. That's why I fuck with you."

They dapped each other up and parted ways.

Malik D. Rice

The sun was gone but the cold winds remained, so Handsome was confused when he saw somebody swinging on a swing set on the playground in the back of the apartments. He was walking from Dreek's apartment, on the way to his own.

He didn't know why he was so curious to know who it was on the swing set, but the fact that it wasn't a child had him wondering. "Kamya?" he asked as he got closer. "Is that you?"

She swung forward, backward, and stopped the next forward swing by planting her feet firmly on the ground. "Who's that?" she asked while squinting her eyes. He was dressed in all-black with a ski-mask on that covered half of his face, so she couldn't tell who it was.

Handsome pulled the ski mask down and closed the distance between them. "What you doing out here in the cold girl?" he asked worriedly.

"Hey, Handsome!" she greeted excitedly before running up to him and hugging him. She loved him just like every other girl he knew.

He held her at arms-length. "What you doing out here like this, Mya? You trying to get sick?"

"No, Babie was smoking that stinky weed in the house so I just came out here to play until it airs out."

He sighed while shaking his head. "You want to wait in my spot? Because I'm not about to let you stay out here, man."

"Ain't that big booty girl staying with you?" she asked with raised eyebrows.

"Man, I kicked her out like three days ago."

"Why?"

"Caught her putting period blood in my ravioli."

She made a nasty face. "Ewwww! Why she do that?"

"Come on, I'll tell you on the way," he said while leading her to his apartment.

34

Three minutes later, they walked inside Handsome's neat apartment. "That's nasty, I wouldn't do that to nobody," Kamya said while standing up awkwardly in the living room.

"I know you wouldn't because you got morals, most people don't." He sat down on the couch after taking off his jacket. "You gon' stand there looking crazy? Or you gon' sit down?" he asked jokingly.

"All the girls always say you ain't no good, and all you good for, is hurting people."

"You want to know why I hurt them?" She nodded her head sheepishly. "Because they ain't no good they damn selves. Have I ever been mean to you?" She shook her head. "Exactly, that's because I know you a good girl. I would never hurt you, Kamya."

That had to be all the motivation she needed because she walked over and took a seat on the couch next to him. "You got on-demand movies on your TV?"

He picked the remote up off the table and handed it to her. "Order whatever you want. You hungry?"

She shook her head. "Nah, I cooked an early dinner."

"Wish I had somebody to cook for me. I had to go all the way to Dreek's house to eat a cooked meal."

She looked over at him sadly with her pretty, hazel eyes. "You can come over to my place and eat. I cook breakfast every morning before school, lunch after school, and dinner before we go to sleep. Well, before I go to sleep. Babie stays up all night most of the time."

"I appreciate that, Mya." He looked over at her in a new light. For the first time, he wasn't looking at her as Rampage's little sister, he saw her as the young woman she was.

He didn't think she knew how beautiful she was. She had pretty eyes, smooth, light-skin, long real hair, and a beautiful personality to go with it all. That, on top of the fact that she was more-than-likely the only virgin in Georgia her age, made her perfect in his eyes. How the hell had he not steered her way before? Well, Rampage was definitely a huge roadblock, but he wasn't there anymore. The road to her heart was clear now.

***

"Toe-Tag be killing me with these random ass missions. I was just knee-deep in some pussy," Quay complained.

Handsome nodded his head. "I was just kicking it with, Kamya. I'm thinking about getting with her."

Everybody stopped dead in their tracks and looked back at him.

"What?"

"Kamya? You dead ass wrong for that. You break that girl's heart, and Toe-Tag gon' have you whacked," Dreek assured matter-a-factly.

Handsome waved him off. "Ain't nobody gon' have me whacked because I'm really fucking with her. I ain't gon' hurt her. I'm gon' treat her right."

Quay and Dreek burst out in laughter.

"What's so funny?" he asked with a straight face.

"Nothing! Let's go pick this lil' nigga up, clean up, and get up out of here," Quay said as they continued walking down an alley off Flat Shoals road.

They neared the red shed that Monster had described to them. Quay opened the door to the shed, and quickly put an arm over his nose to suppress the foul smell of death that came escaping out of the shed.

Razor sat on the shed floor that was covered in a pool of blood with a knife in one hand, and a gun in the other.

"I guess he cut they throats with the knife and blew his own brain's out with the Glock," Quay analyzed before picking up his phone, making a call.

"What?" Monster answered with his usual aggression.

"Nigga, you said it was gon' be two bodies to clean up. I'm standing here looking at three."

"What you talking about? The lil' nigga, Razor, dead?"

Quay nodded even though Monster couldn't see him. "By the looks of things, it looks like he put the gun up under his chin and pulled the trigger."

He heard Monster tell Toe-Tag what happened, then he heard a series of laughter follow. "Babie talking about that lil' nigga was built for this shit! I knew he wasn't no killer when I looked in his eyes, but oh well, fuck it. Clean the lil' nigga up, too. I'll pay y'all a lil' extra."

Quay took the phone away from his ear and looked at it. "A lil' extra? Nigga, you gon' pay two-gees for him just like the other two, or you can bring yo' big ass back down here and scoop him up yourself."

Monster chuckled. "I had to try, go ahead, though. I got y'all. Just hurry up because the sun comes up in about four more hours."

"All I need is three." He promised before ending the call and placing the phone back in his pocket.

"Wassup?" asked Handsome.

Quay looked at him with his game face. "Go get the van and pull it around here. We got three bodies and a lake of blood to clean up in three hours. Let's get it!"

Handsome went for the van while Dreek helped him lay plastic down just outside the shed entrance so they could carry the first body onto it. In their line-of-work, they made messes most of the time, but sometimes, they had to clean the shit up, too.

Malik D. Rice

CHAPTER 5

"What you got on your mind lil' nigga?" Monster asked Toe-Tag who sat in the back of the truck with him.

"Thinking of a master plan."

Monster laughed. "Nahhh, you lying. Shawty on yo' mind!"

"Shut the fuck up," he spat playfully unable to hold back his smile. "Shanay, be on a nigga mind too, but not right now. I'm really trying to make this shit work. Most Dons in our camp don't last long. I'm trying to be the one to grow old on this throne."

Monster nodded. "I feel you. What you got in mind?"

"All type of shit, but we got to get Vonte out the way first, then everything else will follow."

"You know your brother proud of you right?"

"Yeah, he tells me every time I talk to him. I hope he gets that appeal."

"Me too."

"We're here," Valencia informed cheerfully. Ever since Toe-Tag had hired her to be his driver, she felt important and appreciated.

They were parked in the parking lot behind KINKY. It was 6:30 a.m., so the partygoers were either sleep, or on their way home, but the staff was still there wrapping the place up to be closed. Not an ideal time for a meeting, but Toe-Tag still called one anyway.

They walked in from the back door and greeted, Mumbo the head of security. He was a mountain of a man with a thick African accent. "Your associates have been waiting on you for a short while." He led them to the first VIP room on the left.

Pablo sat on one of the sofas lazily with three of his men on the other. "Looks like y'all niggas had a long night?" said Toe-Tag as he walked in with Monster.

"I hope this shit is good? You called me all the way out here in the middle of the night. It took me two hours to get here," Pablo complained.

"It's not my fault you chose to stay so far away from the hood. Y'all let me talk to Pablo alone." He waited until everybody left before taking a seat on the opposite sofa.

"What you got on your mind, Toe-Tag?"

"Success."

Pablo looked at him blankly. "Please get to the point."

"Vonte got to go," he spat bluntly.

Pablo's blank face turned into a mask of shock, and confusion. "I'm gon' pretend like I ain't hear that."

"Nigga, you hear because I want you to hear it."

"Let me guess, you gon' kill Vonte, and take his spot?" he asked sarcastically. "Like they do in the old mafia movies."

"Nah, I'm gon' kill him and you gon' take his spot."

"Talk to me," Pablo said with much more interest.

Four hours later, Pablo was sitting in Vonte's loft. "The little nigga got big plans," he informed jokingly.

"I see. Did he say anything else?" Vonte asked without taking his focus off the solid gold, and platinum, chessboard he played on with Silent.

Pablo shook his head causing his dreads to sway with it. "Not really, just the fact that this camp ain't big enough for the both of y'all."

Silent castled his king and laughed.

"That lil' nigga crazy ain't he, bro'?" Vonte asked Silent amusingly. "I was gon' let the lil' nigga rock for at least a year, or two, but now he just shortened the fuck out of his time."

New to the Game 2

Silent grabbed his M-14 off the floor, stood up out of his chair, and prepared to leave.

"Not now, Silent. Go snatch up his whole family."

Silent gave him a knowing look.

"Yes, I'm sure. Round up the kill-team, and round his family up. Then text me when everything is good."

Silent nodded his head and left.

"That nigga gives me the chills," Pablo said once Silent was gone.

Vonte smiled. "Me too. You know how to play chess?"

***

Papa was the head Mafioso in Pablo's camp. He was a twenty-six-year-old veteran in the scam game. He walked next to Toe-Tag, in his apartment complex, looking like a college student in his preppy clothing. The only thing that gave him away was the small red-and-blue 'DG' tattooed under his left eye, the only tattoo on his entire body.

"I told you he was going to run back to, Vonte. He's terrified of the nigga."

Toe-Tag nodded his head. "Why you not terrified of him?"

"Never said I wasn't." He walked over to the side of his building and leaned against the cold brick. "I've been hearing about you, and your camp in the streets, and on the news. Vonte's underestimating you, and I just so happen to know the power of underestimation."

Toe-Tag dug his hand's inside his Monclear coat pocket and stopped in front of him. "Pablo got to go, I can't trust no nigga like that."

Papa chuckled softly.

"Fuck is so funny?"

"Y'all young niggas think guns will solve all of your problems. Spare Pablo, he can be useful."

"How?" Toe-Tag asked with an unbelieving face.

He lit a cigarette, puffed twice, and blew a cloud of smoke into the night sky. "Once you handle, Vonte, we'll need somebody to take his spot that can easily be run over. Having Vonte out of the picture, leaves you and that big ass nigga over there for him to be scared of," he said motioning towards, Monster who stood in a dark cut a few yards away from them with his AK-74 in hand looking up-and-down the street for any possible threats.

"Tell me one thing, Papa."

Papa nodded his head for him to continue.

"What's your angle in this?" He looked over at the money green Ferrari that Papa pulled up in. "By the looks of things, you eating good with him. So, why go against him?"

"I just told you not to whack him. I'm not against him. I just think it's time I got a promotion."

Toe-Tag eyed him up-and-down. "You know what'll happen if I even get the urge to think about you crossing me, right?"

"Come on, youngster. You got to trust somebody."

"The only nigga I trust is that big ass nigga over there," he informed before walking off ending their short meeting.

New to the Game 2

CHAPTER 6

"At least your nigga still alive," Babie told Kamya sadly as she balled up even tighter on the couch. She looked younger than her age in the one-piece American flag printed pajama suit.

"You don't know if Razor's dead. And Handsome isn't my nigga, we're just talking," Kamya corrected after drawing her in for a big hug.

Babie looked up at her through slanted eyes. "I asked Monster what happened to him. He said that Razor couldn't be Loyal 4 Eva. That's damn-near the same shit Toe-Tag told me when Raylo died. I'm starting to figure out the meaning—and girl you should know better. If Handsome looks at you for more than ten seconds, you belong to him. Every bitch in East Atlanta knows that."

"I just hope, he don't hurt me, Babie."

"Yeah, right. That nigga knows better. Toe-Tag will cut his dick off personally if he thinks about hurting you. So, if he's showing interest in you, he must got plans on doing right by you."

A look of pure hope flashed on Kamya's face. "You really think so?"

"I know so." She pulled out her phone and clicked on a porno flick. "Now, you need to watch-and-learn because I heard that nigga got a big dick, and he knows how to use it!"

Kamya pushed the phone away. "Stoppp, Babie!"

"Nah, bitch! You want to be grown, you gon' have to put that pussy on him like you grown!" she spat playfully while chasing Kamya around their apartment with the phone.

***

"Mooski, wake your muthafuckin' ass up! Every time I come back to the house, you got all these niggas, and bitches, in my shit. Why the fuck you ain't in school?"

Mooski had just gone to sleep not even a full two hours ago. He must've lost track of the days because he didn't know his uncle would be back today. His uncle was a long-distance truck driver and left the spot for weeks at a time, leaving him plenty of time to do his thing.

"I got kicked out last semester," he informed groggily and rolled over in the bed.

His uncle walked up to his bed and snatched the covers off him. "You gon' get you a job, or something if you want to stay in this apartment."

"I already got a job," he informed as he sat up on the bed and ran a hand through his dreaded Mohawk.

"Dilluminati don't sign paychecks."

"Shittin' me."

"The rent is four-fifty. I need half of that if you want to stay here."

He smiled wickedly. What his uncle didn't know is that the same niggas he'd just put out of the apartment just went with Mooski on a caper.

"Oh, yeah?" He got up, dug in the left pocket of his True Religion jeans, and came out with a healthy bankroll. "Here, take five-hundred. Buy you some lunch or some shit with the extra."

His uncle was speechless for the first time and just walked out with the money in his hand.

Mooski got dressed and left the apartment. He was walking through the neighborhood on the way to his partner's spot to go play the game when Babie called out to him from her upstairs window. "Why you ain't in school, lil' boy?"

"I got kicked out, you know that."

She shook her head. "Yo' badass, I heard about that shit you did last night."

"Oh, yeah?" he asked with a sly smirk. News traveled so fast in their hood it wasn't even funny. "Don't listen to everything you hear."

She rolled her eyes. "Nigga, please. Where you going?"

"About to go play the game at Gutta's spot."

"You want to play the game with me? I still got Rampage's PS4 in here."

He thought about it with other, more lustful plans on his mind.

"Nah, he can't. Toe-Tag needs to holla at him real quick," Dreek said walking up out of nowhere.

Babie smiled down at them. "If Toe-Tag sent him for you, that means you going places in this lil' world of ours. I'm proud of you. You gon' hit me up later on?"

"I got you," he assured before walking off with Dreek.

"You need to stay away from her. That lil' pussy right there is cursed," Dreek warned as they cut through a building on the way to Toe-Tag's spot.

He laughed.

"I'm trying to tell you what's going on, but I already know you hardheaded. So, go ahead and learn the hard way."

He waved him off. Dreek's black ass was always warning somebody about one thing, or another. He'd been trying to fuck Babie's little high-maintenance ass for months, and he'd be damned if he'd pass up his chance now that he was finally getting some recognition.

"What the Don want with me?"

"You'll see."

Toe-Tag, and Monster, was in the living room watching the Atlanta Hawks play the Milwaukee Bucks. They had everything from guns, snacks, to drugs on the table, and they both wore Hawks jerseys over their hoodies.

Mooski took a peek at the TV and saw that the Hawks were up by five points. He nodded his head approvingly. He was a Hawks fan himself he had the logo tatted big on the front of his neck. It was the only tattoo he had other than the DG on his forehead with an upside-down cross right up under it.

"Sit down, nigga," Toe-Tag instructed without taking his eyes off the game.

He took a seat on the other couch with Dreek. "Wassup?" he asked.

He was only a year younger than Toe-Tag and used to hang with him on a daily basis at one point of time, but they grew distant once Toe-Tag started going up in rank, now he felt uneasy around him.

Toe-Tag grabbed a pack of Starburst off the table, then looked at him brightly. "You tell me, I heard about that work you put in yesterday. That's the type of shit that gets you put on my kill-team."

Last night Mooski decided to take down a small crew of weed dealers on the outskirts with a few Young Mobsters from the hood. They didn't scope the spot out how they were supposed to and didn't know that the ringleader of the operation kept two shooters in the stash spot. They kicked the door in thinking that nobody was there until the shooters opened fire on them in the house. Everybody else took cover, but Mooski psyched-out and took them down by himself.

"How much y'all make off that move?"

"About twenty pounds of weed, and forty-grand. We split the forty for ten-grand apiece."

Toe-Tag nodded impressively. "What y'all do with the weed?"

New to the Game 2

"We got nineteen of them at Gutta's spot. We was gon' give it to you to pay our dues."

"I'm straight, you keep that to yourself since you put in most of the work."

He nodded his head in understanding.

"You trying to get with the kill-team?"

If only he knew how long he'd been waiting to hear those words. "Come on, bro'. What nigga in this camp don't want to be on the kill-team?"

"Good answer," Toe-Tag said before reaching onto the table, grabbing an iced-out white gold DG choke chain, and tossing it on Mooski's lap. "You a Mafioso now. Follow orders, keep your gun off safety, and you gon' make it."

For a shooter in their camp, making the Dons kill-team was like signing a record deal for a rapper. He had just become royalty, and wanted to jump for joy, but had to hold his composure. He looked down at the icy chain in his hand and could tell that the diamonds were real, none of the Mafioso's wore fake jewelry. "I appreciate this right here, my loyalty is 4 Eva."

Monster looked over at him. "It better be. You ready to put in some work for the Don?"

"I was born for this shit."

Malik D. Rice

CHAPTER 7

Ronte had a show at a big ass club in downtown Houston, Texas, and nearly begged Vonte to come. Although they were twin brothers Vonte always acted as the big brother since he was more aggressive, and naturally grew up faster.

"I'm glad you came, man. All this nigga wants to talk about is, Vonte-this-Vonte-that," Ronte's top shooter, Fifty informed Vonte jokingly. He was a big, brown-skinned man that made his weight look good.

Ronte threw a Fiji water bottle at Fifty. "Shut the fuck up!"

They were backstage waiting for the owner to tell them when it was time to hit the stage.

"Oh, yeah?" Vonte asked amusingly. "You hear that, Facts? My lil' nigga bragging about me," He told his friend while bringing Ronte in for a half-hug-half-chokehold.

Ronte struggled to push off him. "Come on, man. You always trying to hug on somebody with yo' gay ass."

Vonte chuckled. "You know you like it. You talk to mamma dumb ass lately?"

"You know it. She blows my phone up more than these groupie bitches. She needs to get back with that young nigga she was fucking with."

Facts laughed at that statement. He was a trusted shooter on Vonte's kill-team.

"What's so funny?" Ronte asked him.

Facts nodded at Vonte.

"What that ugly ass nigga laughing at?" he asked Vonte.

"She can't go back to the young nigga because he's dead."

Ronte made a shocked face looking like a spitting image of his brother without the face tattoos and the long dreads. "Bro', you need to stop your shit. What good is me praying for you if you catching more bodies than the prayers I'm sending up for you?"

"You get paid to rap, not to pray for niggas. Stick to the lyrics lil' bro."

Ronte rocked the show like the superstar he was. The crowd went crazy singing every one of the six songs he performed word-for-word. They handpicked a large group of girls out of the crowd and brought them back to the hotel room for an explicit after party.

"These hoes getting loose. They ain't got no shame in their game," Vonte told his brother while watching a black girl eat her Dominican friend's pussy like it was the best thing she'd ever tasted. "Hoes be going crazy for me, but they be going insane about yo' ugly ass."

Ronte shook his head. "Stupid ass, nigga, I look just like you. And this ain't shit. You should've seen how them hoe's acted in Brazil last week I ain't never seen nothing like it. You know about their AIDS rate over there, right? I was so scared to fuck one of them hoes that I had to jack my dick shawty. It was this one bitch—"

Vonte's business phone vibrated, he had to tune Ronte out for a little bit. He'd been waiting to hear from Silent for a minute, but it wasn't Silent. It was somebody else who'd sent him a picture of Silent tied up in a chair with his dreads shaved off and cigarette burn marks on his head.

"Oh, shit!"

"What happened?" asked Ronte with a worried expression. He knew Vonte wasn't easily rattled, so just by him being worried about something was enough to spark his concern.

Vonte looked at him with soulless eyes. "I got to go, but I need you to do me a favor."

"Anything."

"Stay your ass out of Atlanta for a few days."

Ronte nodded rattling the three single, red-white-blue, dreads that stopped just above his left eye. He knew better than to ask Vonte any questions. "My tour don't bring me back to Atlanta for another week and some change."

"Good, because shit about to get ugly out there."

***

Kapo laid in his bed watching a documentary on the Notorious Kingpin, Pablo Escobar on his 75-inch TV that hung high on his bedroom wall. Those federal agents handed his ass to him. He made a mental note to never spit in one of their faces again. He wasn't worried about the assault charges because his lawyer would get them dropped, but he still had to be careful because they were all over his ass.

He was just blessed that he came out with a busted lip, fractured jaw, black eye, minor concussion, and a few bruised ribs. Compared to the ass whooping they put on Rampage, and Black, he was lucky not to have any broken bones. He was scheduled to be back up and running in no time. The quicker he got back to it, the faster he could find out who the fuck killed his sweet, little, baby girl. He'd been having nightmares and sinister thoughts ever since the incident, and to make things worse, his wife turned her back on him when he needed her the most. She blamed him for Kandice's death and lost all love for him. As bad as he wanted to lose years-and-years' worth of love for her, he couldn't. A part of him would always love her, but at the same time, a part of him could never forgive her for what she did.

"Boss, I know you told us not to disturb you, but there's a young man by the name of Toe-Tag requesting to see you," Bullet informed with his head stuck inside the bedroom door.

Kapo sat up a little bit. "Where? He's here?"

"Yes."

"How the fuck did he know where I lived?" Kapo asked before remembering that he'd had Rampage over his house before, who probably told Toe-Tag where he stayed. "Never mind. Where is he?"

"In the BMW truck that he pulled up in. There's a young woman in the driver's seat, and another young male in the back with Toe-Tag. Would you like for them to be terminated?" he asked seriously.

Kapo hired extra security and has been on high alert ever since he'd come home from the hospital. Kapo shook his head frantically. "No, don't terminate them. Go bring him to me, alone."

Toe-Tag tried to pass Mooski his iPhone with a line of cocaine on the screen. "Nah, I'm good bro'. I'm good with the weed."

"You spend enough time on the kill-team, and you gon' need some of this shit just to feel like you alive. Enjoy that the lil' soul while you got it, nigga," he informed before vacuuming the line up his nose.

"That white man walking back down the driveway," Valencia informed from the driver's seat.

Mooski gripped his MP4, and Toe-Tag cleaned his nose with a piece of tissue.

The white guard knocked on the back window, and Mooski let it down for him. "He wants to see you alone," he informed while looking at Toe-Tag before walking back up the driveway and posting up in the front with two more serious-looking guards.

Toe-Tag tucked his 40. Caliber in his waistband. "If I don't come out in ten minutes, call me. If I don't answer, drive back to the hood, come back with *everybody* and kill all these fuck niggas," he commanded before getting out of the truck.

Valencia sighed deeply once he was gone.

"What?" asked Mooski.

"I think I'm in love with him."

He just shook his head.

"You just showed up on the Pope's doorstep unannounced. I can take your stripes just for that," Kapo told Toe-Tag while sitting up in his bed staring daggers at the young executioner who stood in his doorway. He tried to take a seat on Kapo's chair, but Kapo stopped him. "Nah, just stand up. This meeting ain't gon' be too long. Now tell me what was so important that you came all this way unannounced."

Toe-Tag looked at Glock and Bullet, who stood statue-still behind him, then back at Kapo. "You might want to hear this in private."

Kapo nodded his head, and they took two steps backward before closing the door.

"Talk."

Toe-Tag pulled his phone out. "You'll be better off listening."

"What the hell kind of games you playing lil' nigga?"

"Just be quiet and listen man."

He went to a voice recording app on his phone, and pulled the curtains back, revealing the truth for Kapo. He came up with the idea to record the conversation that he had with Vonte a few days ago when they were in the back of his Bentley.

Kapo sat there listening to the short conversation, and his light face was getting redder-and-redder by the second. By the time the recording was finished, Toe-Tag honestly thought that he wasn't going to make it out of the house by the way Kapo was glaring at him. Tears were flowing down his face freely, and his breathing had picked up dramatically.

"Don't be mad at me. He threatened my whole family. I tried to buck on the hit, but he made me do it."

Kapo just put his face in his hands and sobbed quietly for a few minutes. Toe-Tag just stood there patiently letting him go through the motions.

"I got one-hundred thousand dollars for you to bring that nigga to me," Kapo spat with a now raspy voice.

Toe-Tag smiled inwardly. "For one-hundred thousand gees, I'll literally bring you his head in a bag with the dreads still attached," he informed seriously.

"Nah, I just need you to snatch the nigga up. I'll kill him myself."

"A'ight," Toe-Tag agreed before turning to leave.

"Wait!" Toe-Tag turned around. "I got one more job for you too, but this one is in witness protection, and you might have to kill a few U.S Marshals to get to them, so I got five-hundred thousand dollars for this target right here."

"I'm gon' need half of the ticket upfront for that job there."

Kapo nodded his head. "Cool, I'll have it delivered to you tonight. Just make sure you don't fuck this up. If you don't think you can pull the job off, let me know now because I'll get somebody else to handle it. If you fuck up on this job, I'll be paying somebody to come whack you."

"Just chill, nigga, I got this shit."

"Good."

"Who the fuck is the target anyway, somebody in DG?"

"Nah, it's my wife."

CHAPTER 8

Toe-Tag's mother, Phat opened the door for him. "Boy, I should beat your muthafuckin' ass! You been—"

"Move, ma! You can curse a nigga out in the house, it's cold as fuck out here." He spat as he rushed past his mother into the house with Mooski, and Valencia on his heels. It was a cold night with high winds and temperatures below freezing. "I see you been decorating this bitch," he noted while looking around the mini mansion he had rented for his family in Gwinett County.

Phat slapped him in the back of the head. "Boy don't be changing the subject. First, you move me, and Terri out of our apartment. We got comfortable there. Then, not only did you move us to this house, you got Shanay and both of her parents in here. Everybody scared for their life thinking goons gon' come busting in this bitch looking for you any second! What the hell you got going on, boy?"

"Ma, just chill! I moved y'all out here so y'all ain't got to worry about nobody trying to do nothing to y'all. Plus, I'm about to eliminate the threat anyway."

Terri came running in the hall looking like a small version of Toe-Tag, just prettier. "Heyyyyy, brother! I'm glad you ain't dead yet!"

"Yet?" He looked down at her with a scrunched face. "Why you say that?"

"Mamma said you gon' die soon."

He looked at their mother through squinted eyes. "Yo' mamma don't know what the fuck she talking about."

Phat rolled her eyes.

"Where Shanay at?" he asked Terri.

"Upstairs sleep with Lil' Tee."

He patted her on the head and made his way upstairs. He hadn't seen Shanay since she left him in the apartment a few weeks ago. He'd text her every once-and-a-while, letting her know how much he loved and missed her, but she would never text back. He never put up a fuss though because he knew she was better off without him.

Just like Terri had told him, they were in the second room to the left, but they both weren't sleep. Lil' Tee was sitting up on the bed watching Adult Swim on Cartoon Network while helping himself to a drink of apple juice from his sippy-cup.

He looked over at Toe-Tag. It took a few seconds for him to recognize his father, but once he did, he started crawling towards the edge of the bed with a big smile on his face.

Toe-Tag grabbed him and picked him up right before he fell off the bed. "Wassup, lil' nigga? You missed yo' daddy?"

"Daddy!" he blurted out waking Shanay straight up out of her sleep.

"Tevin?" she asked groggily. She'd been dreaming about him so much lately, she didn't know if this was one, or not, but after a few seconds, she knew it was real. "Tevin!" She jumped up and gave him a big hug.

"Damn, if you missed a nigga. Why you ain't just hit my line?" he asked while looking down at her sexy body in the pink skintight Victoria's Secret sweatsuit she wore.

She pushed off him. "Because I'm still mad at you, but I'm glad your stupid ass ain't dead yet."

"Damn. What the fuck wrong with y'all folks? I ain't going nowhere."

She sucked her teeth. "Rampage told Jasmine, and his sisters, the same shit the same night he got whacked. I'm just preparing myself for the inevitable. That is why you been acting so careless, right? Because you know yo' time ain't gon' be long?"

Toe-Tag put Lil' Tee down. "I ain't come here for all that shit. I just wanted to see my lil' nigga and drop some money off." He tossed a bankroll on the bed and began to walk out of the room.

"Bye, daddy!" Lil Tee called after him.

He turned around and saw Lil' Tee sitting on the bed waving at him.

"Don't say bye, son. I'll see you later."

***

"I found out the source of all your problems—our problems," Kapo informed while puffing on a thumb-sized blunt of exotic weed. He'd stopped smoking a few years back but had just started back recently. He didn't want a clear mind anymore.

After his little meeting with Toe-Tag, he found the strength to get up and get to it. The only thing that would keep him from self-destructing was working. He had to suck himself as far inside of the underworld as possible. He would be the most powerful Pope that there was.

"Oh, yeah?" Freddy asked while sitting on the other side of Kapo's desk in his home office. "Talk to me."

He made Toe-Tag send him a copy of the audio recording of them just so he could play it for Freddy. After the recording was over, he stared at Freddy with an expecting look.

"What?"

"Fuck you mean *what*? You need to find you another Underboss for the Eastside because his ass is gone. That nigga was *never* Loyal 4 Eva."

Freddy took a very deep breath. He loved Ronte, but Vonte had always been his favorite nephew. He protected him as much as he could, but there was nothing he could do about it now. Vonte had fucked up big this time. "I'll handle it."

Kapo shook his head. "Nah, I got it. The hit already been put out. I just need you to find another Underboss ASAP." He really wanted to whack Freddy just because they were so close and looked alike.

"Cool," he assured before getting up and leaving Kapo's house.

Freddy had apartments, houses, and condos throughout Atlanta. Some he rented, some he let his girlfriends' stay in, and some he just kept vacant for emergency placements, such as this one.

"Listen, unc', I'm not about to stay in this house hiding like no lil' bitch! Let Kapo send whoever the fuck he wants. Me and my kill-team gon' take 'em down!" Vonte vented while pacing the dining room floor.

Freddy was at the table trying to enjoy a Caribbean meal he'd prepared himself, but Vonte was making it difficult. "You in this predicament now because of your hardheaded-ness. I told you time-and-time again, that you can't be out here moving reckless, now look at you. You trying to go up against the whole Dilluminati. I can't save you his time, nephew."

"I don't need your saving, nigga. I got plenty of niggas willing to go against the grain for me. I got an army of my own," he boasted with his chest out.

Freddy just nodded his head. Ronte took after their mother's personality, but Vonte reminded him of their father, EJ. He was one of the biggest gun-traffickers on the East coast until he got whacked by the Russian Mafia for stepping on their toes. That was Freddy's only brother, and Vonte was the closest thing he had to him. He couldn't lose Vonte.

"I just need you to lay low until I can get you out of the country."

Vonte looked at him like he was the one with the mental health issues, and not the other way around. "I thought you knew me better than that. I don't care if they do kill me, but it won't happen before I put Kapo, and that fuck nigga Toe-Tag in the dirt!" he spat before putting his trench coat on, grabbing his gun, and storming out.

Freddy didn't even attempt to stop him. He kind of knew shit was going to play out like this, but he had to at least try. All he could do was pray for his nephew even though he doubted God would listen to anything he had to say about Vonte.

Malik D. Rice

CHAPTER 9

"Big Keisha requested to get Black whacked," Monster informed Toe-Tag as they sat in his apartment counting the $250,000 Kapo had delivered.

Toe-Tag stopped in mid-count. "Why? That's crazy."

"She blames him for G-Baby's death. You must ain't heard what she did to that nigga the other day?"

"Man, you know I been in my own world lately. What happened?"

Monster sat the stack of money he was counting down and lit a cigarette. "This crazy-ass bitch went to, Black's apartment while his baby mother went on a run to the store and fucked him up bad. Kicked him in the ribs, pistol-whipped him, and all. That nigga fucked up all over again. He was just starting to heal."

Toe-Tag cringed just thinking about the pain Black was going through. "Damn, shit ruff out here in the jungle. Everybody savages around this bitch."

"That's all we know. What you want me to tell her?"

"Tell her if she touches Black again, *she* gon' get whacked."

Monster laughed at Toe-Tag's madness. "You got a plan for this hit?"

"Got to pay at least fifty gees for her location, and we just gon' have to lay from there. We gon' have to be patient and wait for the perfect timing. As long as she gets whacked before Kapo's trial, we good. She all they got."

"What about, Vonte?"

Toe-Tag took a deep breath. "I don't know. He got a lot of pressure on him right now, though. He'll split up; I just want him dead. I don't care if we do it, or somebody else."

"Sound about right." He checked his iPhone watch. "It's about that time for me to handle that other shit for you."

Toe-Tag nodded. "Go ahead, I'll get finished counting this shit. Take Handsome and Mooski, with you. Them niggas think they slick fucking around with Kamya and Babie."

"I got you, bro'." Monster stated while laughing his way out the door.

The word got out fast about Vonte's deceit, replacement, and pending termination. Not only in the city of Atlanta but state-to-state. Vonte was labeled a traitor and DG shooters were ordered to kill-on-sight. It was only right for Freddy to bump, Pablo up to the Underboss over the Eastside, and of course, Pablo bumped, Papa up to the Don over his previous camp.

Pablo was having a small celebration with his family at his mansion in Monroe, Georgia. His wife, kids, mother, siblings, and a few friends all showed up to congratulate him for his success.

He sat at the head of the long oak wood table that sat in his beautiful dining room enjoying the meal when one of his new security guards came and whispered something in his ear, then walked off. He dismissed himself with a smile so anyone wouldn't be alerted, buttoned up his peak coat, and walked out the front door.

At the bottom of his stairs sitting in his wrap-a-round driveway was a black Escalade with two young shooters dressed in all black standing in front of it facing him.

"How long have they been here?" he asked his guard.

"They just arrived not too long ago, requesting you. Don Toe-Tag, if I'm not mistaken."

He walked toward the truck with huge butterflies in his stomach. He was flat-out scared, but he had to keep his composure. One of the shooters opened the back door as he approached. He climbed in and saw Monster sitting alone in the back.

"Pablo, I knew you was living good, my nigga, but damn! I might have to get me some of that scam money."

"Where's Toe-Tag? How did y'all find out where I live?"

Monster smiled devilishly. "You'll be surprised what kind of information you can get out of a muthafucka that knows you whack shit for a living."

"What do you want?"

"I'm just the messenger."

"What does Toe-Tag want then?"

"If he ever needs a favor, you need to be there."

"What he needs?"

Monster shrugged his shoulders. "You'll know when he needs it."

***

Vonte looked around the basement in disgust. There were only two shooters, out of twenty, that stood by his side. The rest of them were scared to go against Dilluminati and followed suit. "I fed *all* them fuck niggas, and this how they do me?"

Facts sat on the floor playing with his grey-eyed Bulldog. They were at one of his fat girl's spots that he made home from time-to-time. "You should've known that. I'm surprised that this nigga, Millie, is here," he said bluntly. He was the closest thing to a father-figure that Vonte had other than, Freddy and planned on riding with the young fearless nigga to the end.

Millie was a young nigga from the hood that was two years older than Vonte but looked up to him like a big brother. He was Venezuelan and Greek. He kept his long silky black hair pulled up in a messy bun making him look like a Vampire. His parents had dropped him off at a foster home when he was a child, and he met Vonte in juvenile. Vonte was the closest thing to family he ever really had.

"Stop playing with me, Facts! Nigga, you know I'll ride and die for, Vonte," he said after jumping down from the pool table.

"Sit yo' ass back down, Millie. I ain't never doubt you, and that's what matters," Vonte stated before turning to Facts. "Stop being a dickhead."

Facts shrugged with a smug smirk on his scarred face.

"What's the plan? We can't go up against Dilluminati with three niggas," Millie asked, then stated.

Vonte paced the floor a few more times before answering. "We gon' have to take a trip to New Orleans."

"Awww-shit!" Facts whined knowingly.

"Awww, my ass. Desperate times cause for desperate measures."

Facts looked at him seriously this time. "You sure about this?"

"We ain't got no choice."

"What the hell are y'all talking about?" Millie asked in frustration.

"You'll see," Vonte and Facts, answered in unison.

CHAPTER 10

"How can somebody be so beautiful, and so dangerous at the same time?" Kamya asked Handsome seriously.

He looked at her awkwardly. "Ain't no way, shawty."

"What?"

"I done been called everything in the book, but beautiful. That's a first," he admitted. "But you know I ain't no bad person, I just came up ruff. You know how the hood is."

She nodded. "I know, but don't you ever think about having kids and raising a family like a regular person?"

"Girl, bye! That nigga on the kill-team. Toe-Tag ain't gon' let that nigga do no shit like that," Babie blurted out rudely. They were all in the living room, so she didn't have a choice but to hear them.

Toe-Tag threw a pillow at her. "Shut yo' ass up lil' girl. Mooski needs to come get yo' ass."

"I got that nigga ass in the bed knocked out. This pussy put his ass straight to sleep," she bragged while patting her love-box through her Gucci jeans.

"Babieeee, get out!" Kamya commanded embarrassingly.

Babie raised her hands in surrender and stood up. "You need to kill all that fairytale shit. If you plan on fucking with that nigga there, you gon' be a mob wife. So, you need to get used to this lifestyle," she warned Kamya before leaving them alone in the living room.

"So, I guess you can't have no regular life, huh?" she asked sadly.

"Want me to let you in on a secret?" She nodded her head. "If I told Toe-Tag I wanted to marry you, take care of you, and get you out the hood, he would give me a pass. Not because of me, and not because of you, but because he knows

Rampage would've wanted you to be happy," he informed matter-a-factly.

She lit up like a Christmas tree. "For real?"

"Yup."

"Why you want to be with me? I'm just a stupid girl from the hood. You got all them foreign pretty girls with big booties chasing you on Instagram."

He lifted her chin up with his index finger and looked her dead in the eyes. "You not stupid. Stop saying that shit and all that should matter is that you're the prettiest girl in my eyes right now," he said before leaning in and kissing her passionately.

She was so pure, and innocent. He was the exact opposite. That's probably why they went so well together. "Promise me one thing, Handsome," she said after pulling her lip's away from his.

"Wassup?"

"I'm not going to rush you to jump out of the game because I know it's not that easy. Just promise to always be here for me, and to never hurt me."

"I promise," he assured before leaning back in for another kiss. Her innocence, and submissive nature, was turning him on, *big time*.

***

Papa dropped a brown paper bag filled with twenties on the pool table. They were at the pool hall right across the street from the club Nite-Lite off Moreland Avenue. "That's forty-grand like we agreed."

Toe-Tag picked the bag up and looked inside with suspicion. "This better not be counterfeit. I know how y'all niggas rock." Papa had offered to pay him in $75,000 counterfeit instead of the $40,000 real money.

"Come on, bro'. You know I wouldn't do you like that."

"I don't know shit. It's play-for-keeps out here, I got to be careful. Anyway, I told you the plan was gon' work. You the top Don, Pablo the Underboss, and I got Vonte's pussy ass out the way."

Papa took a seat on the pool table and sat where he could keep an eye on this thick model chick he was obsessed with these days. "He's out the way, but he's not gone yet, and that bothers me."

"Well, Silent is gone, and all of his shooters running to me for a home. He ain't shit without 'em. His ass gon' get it soon enough," he assured confidently.

Papa nodded his understanding. "Is that a new piece?" He was looking down at the brightest chain on Toe-Tag's neck. It had the word *TOE* with a real toe tag hanging up under the *O*.

Toe-Tag looked down at his neck, and back up at his associate. "You worried about the wrong thing, old school," he retorted before grabbing the paper bag off the table and walking out with Monster on his heels.

"Old school?" Papa asked himself with a confused expression. "Since when is twenty-six old school? These young niggas is out of hand," he concluded before calling his girl over to him.

Dead Shot was on Vonte's notorious kill-team and was now acting as the leader for the rest of them. He was in his mid-twenties, about 180 pounds, standing at 5'9. He was a bull of a nigga with the type of aggression that you needed to be running with Vonte for as long as he did. Now he was standing there facing another young bull trying to get on his kill-team.

Toe-Tag found it amusing how most of the young niggas in Dilluminati had the power. Wasn't it supposed to be the other way around? Young niggas were taking over the game, and nobody could stop it.

They tried to pull up on Pablo to get on his kill-team, but he preferred professional security, and the rest of the Dons didn't need him on their kill-team, so they had to come to Toe-Tag since he ran a camp full of shooters. It was only right.

The shooters listened to Dead-Shot, but he wasn't a mademan, so there he was standing face-to-face with Toe-Tag in a large patch of woods in Covington, Georgia.

"Why you call me all the way out here, by myself?"

"Because I don't trust you. Now, can you pull the job off, or not? A mistake gon' cost you your life," Toe-Tag informed with his hands shoved deep in the pocket of his Armani trench coat. It seemed to be getting colder-and-colder by the day.

"Young nigga, I been doing this shit since you was in elementary, I got this."

"Since your name is Dead Shot, make sure it's a headshot," he commanded jokingly.

Dead Shot laughed at his bad joke. "It'll get done."

"You do four free missions for me, and you start getting paid for the ones after. You know how this shit go."

"Say less, that's all," he said impatiently ready to get going.

Toe-Tag shook his head. "Nah, I got something I need you to do first. This will count as the first mission."

"What?"

Toe-Tag pointed his index finger to the sky and twirled it around in a circle. The next thing they knew, the doors to the Escalade behind the BMW opened. Monster and Dreek grabbed a big duffle bag out of the trunk from each end, carried it all the way over to where they stood and dropped it with a thump, then walked back to the truck.

"What's that?" Dead Shot asked curiously while looking down at the big black bag.

Toe-Tag smiled showing his new permanent platinum diamond grill. It was $30,000 well-spent. "That's Silent. Well, pieces of him anyway. Head, arms, legs. Everything's separate, but you don't have to worry about it because I already got the hard part out the way. All the parts are drained and wrapped in plastic, I just need you to get rid of them, in different places of course."

Dead Shot noticed how passionate he spoke when he talked about death, and it didn't go unnoticed. "You not as fucked up as, Vonte, but the fact still remains—you need help, young nigga."

"You can help me by dispersing that body for me, old school," he retorted before walking off towards his Beamer.

Dead Shot scratched the afro on his head and transformed his face into a mask of pure confusion. "Old school?"

Malik D. Rice

CHAPTER 11

Silent's family originally came from a small town in Haiti but migrated to the outskirts of New Orleans in the late eighties. His mother moved to Atlanta for a fresh start in the late nineties, and that's how he got there, but his family continued to build their roots in the city of New Orleans.

His grandfather, Follian had started a demonic cult in the city that made their ends by trafficking Heroin all around the state of Louisiana. After Silent's mother got sick and died from lung cancer, he still kept in touch with his family in New Orleans.

"You think they know that Silent is dead?" Facts asked Vonte while they drove down a very long dirt road paved in the woods.

"Nigga, nobody outside of Dilluminati knows he's dead. He just missing to the rest of the world." That's just how it was most of the time. When a nigga got whacked in Dilluminati chances were you'd never find the body.

Facts shook his head. "And we got to be the ones to tell this nigga that one of his favorite grandson's is dead? I would've felt safer doing this shit over the phone. Silent one crazy ass nigga, but it ain't even no words to describe the rest of his family. The last time we came out here with Silent, he barely stopped them, folks, from killing us, and sacrificing us to the Devil. What the fuck gon' stop these folks this time? Especially since we coming to tell them that the nigga done got whacked for being around us. I ain't scared of nobody lil' bro', but guess what? I don't consider these folks as people," he said with his eyes on the road the whole time.

"How come I ain't never know about Silent's family? Why I ain't come out here with y'all?" Millie asked from the passenger's seat feeling left out. All he knew was that Silent barely talked, to begin with, but after that trip, he took with them, nobody ever heard Silent's voice again.

"Trust me, you was lucky up until now," Vonte assured.

Facts drove the Land Rover to a dead end. There was no more road left.

"What now?" asked Millie.

"We walk the rest of the way," Facts answered while opening his door, and stepping out.

Millie opened his door and saw the mushy mud on the ground. "Oh, hell no! Y'all should've told me about this at the hotel before I stepped out in these Balenciagas."

"Killer, and a pretty boy. One helluva combination. Stay yo' ass in the truck then," Vonte said before leading the way through the woods knowing that he would follow.

"Ughhh! I can't stand these niggas," Millie ranted before hopping out of the truck and following them.

Forty minutes after hiking through the thick woods, they all were exhausted. "We should've just rented a muthafuckin' helicopter. This shit don't make no sense," Millie complained while struggling to keep up.

"If we would've pulled up in a helicopter that muthafucka would've got blown up in the sky before it had a chance to hit the ground. Just chill, we here anyway. You lucky it's still light outside. We took this trip in the middle of the night last time," Facts informed.

Millie looked around, he didn't see a house or anything. He was about to say something until they neared a man-made lake with a big estate on an island right in the middle of it. Everything was built from scratch.

"What the fuck?" Mille said in disbelief. The shit was beautiful. He'd never seen anything like it.

Vonte shrugged. "Shit look different at nighttime. I'm surprised, too."

"Ohhhhh-shit!" They all said in unison as a bullet from a high-powered rifle struck the ground in between them.

"Put y'all hands up and face the island!" Vonte instructed while following his own directions. "Let them see our faces."

"Did y'all get shot at the last time?" Millie asked sarcastically.

Facts shook his head. "When we came out here with Silent it was a boat waiting for us."

They must've recognized Vonte, and Facts because they were still alive, and a rowboat set out on the way towards them. "Here we go," Vonte said unenthusiastically.

Twenty minutes later, they were sitting inside a huge sitting room inside the main mansion on the estate waiting for Mr. Follian to see them.

There was a thick foul scent that hovered in the air throughout the whole compound, and it was killing them.

"If I don't remember nothing else about the last visit, a nigga can't never forget this damn smell," Facts whispered while covering his face with the collar of his peak coat.

"Shhh!" Vonte shushed him as he noticed footsteps on the dark hardwood floor in the hallway.

A tall, slim man with long silver dreads that dropped to the floor walked into the room surrounded by six mean-looking Haitian dudes. You would never be able to tell the man was in his early eighties. He could easily pass for sixty by his skin, and the way he still maneuvered. "Unexpected visits, they're so disrespectful, and can be viewed as a threat." He was very soft-spoken with a thick Caribbean accent.

"It's an urgent matter—I need you Mr. Follian," Vonte informed sincerely. He made sure to keep eye-contact with him because Silent's mother had told him to *always* look a member of his family in the eyes while speaking to them.

"Why should I help you when you let my grandson die?"

All three of them looked at each other, but it was Vonte who spoke, "How did you know?"

"He would've never let you come here alone if he still had breath in his body. I prayed that if anything ever happened to him you would be cursed and forced to come running to me."

Nobody said anything for a long while.

"I'm sorry, I never meant for anything to happen to him. I took good care of him, Mr. Follian."

A muscular man with wild matted dreads puffed his chest out. "You took bad care of him because he's not here!" He was one of Silent's first cousins.

Mr. Follian shushed his grandson. "I know why you're here. You wish to hold the blessings of Satan. Am I correct?" Vonte nodded. "Did you ever find out why Silent never said another word the last visit?" Vonte shook his head. "It was a sacrifice he took to continue being with you."

"What? I don't understand."

"His ancestors tried to make him drop everything he had going on out there in Atlanta with you to come out here and be with his family where he belonged. He disobeyed them, so they forbid him from ever speaking. Do you know why I'm not upset that my grandson died on your watch?"

Vonte shook his head impatiently. He was eager to hear the rest of what the man had to say.

"Because his death was inevitable, you wouldn't have been able to stop it if you tried. He'd strayed away from the path, and the punishment was death. He knew that, but I wonder why he threw his life away for you. I guess you have powerful ancestors as well. I've noticed something special about you since I laid my eyes on you, which is the *only* reason, I'm going to help you today. First, one thing must be done."

"Anything," Vonte agreed desperately. He needed Mr. Follian's help to accomplish his goals.

"You have to sacrifice one of them," he informed while looking at Facts, and Millie with those sharp eagle-eyes of his.

Before either Facts or Millie could get a word out, they both found themselves in chokeholds by very muscular arms. They were pulled up and over their seats on the couch. Both of them were fighting to get free of the submission holds to no avail.

"Come on, Mr. Follian. Is there anything else I can do?"

He shook his head making his long dreads shift. "If you want my help, you'll put this in one of their hearts right now," he stated while placing a super-sharp dagger in Vonte's hand.

Vonte took the dagger and looked over at his two brothers. They were the only two to stand by him against all odds, and now he was forced to kill one of them. He was a cold motherfucker, but everybody had their limits. He couldn't bring himself to do it.

He gave Mr. Follian his dagger back. "I can't do it. You might as well kill me now for wasting your time and let them go. I made them come with me. Don't take it out on them."

Mr. Follian smiled showing his big white teeth. "That was a test young one, and you passed. One thing we value in this family above all else is loyalty. I know my grandson was loyal to you for a reason."

By the time they were making their way back through the woods, it was dark, but Mr. Follian was kind enough to give them flashlights. All they had to do was follow the red ribbons tied to the trees every other yard, or so.

"I ain't gon' lie, nigga, I thought you was gon' whack me," Millie admitted truthfully.

Vonte looked back at him. "What kind of nigga would I be to do some shit like that?"

"I mean I'm glad you ain't do it, but I could've sworn I was dead."

"What now? You just sold your soul to the Devil. What's next?" Facts asked through heavy breaths, he was tired already.

"We gon' lay low and get right. Then when the time's right, we gon' come back harder than ever."

CHAPTER 12

3 Weeks Later

"Where is he, Ciara?" Quay asked Black's favorite baby mother.

She pointed her index finger down the hall. "In the room playing with lil' Vernon. I hope you not coming on no bullshit, Quay. He already been through enough. He just starting to heal inside-and-out."

"Come on, sis. You know I got hella love for, Black. I'm just here to check on the nigga. He been M.I.A for a minute. He ain't answering nobody's calls or nothing."

Ciara nodded her head. You would think she was Black's sister if you didn't know any better. "Okay, he always spoke good things about you, that's why I let you in."

"'Preciate that," he said sincerely and made his way to the back room where the music was playing.

The door was already cracked, so he didn't knock. He just pushed it open. "Yooo!"

Black was on the bed watching Vernon play Grand Theft Auto 5 while puffing away on a joint of weed. He looked up at Quay and had to do a doubletake. He looked Quay up and down and took notice of his new jewelry, and expensive attire. "I see you out there doing good for yourself. Been seeing you flexing on Instagram and shit."

Quay took a seat on the lazy-boy chair in the corner. "Just making this shit look good. You know I'm bad with managing money. This shit going out faster than it's coming in. Vernon, you ain't gone say nothing to yo' uncle?"

"Wassup, Uncle Quay? My bad I was playing the game," he greeted after glancing in Quay's direction.

Black smiled faintly and ruffled his son's hair. "Go kick it with yo' mamma real quick while I chop it up with your uncle."

"Come on, pops! I'm on the way to go rob the bank!"

"Boy, get yo' lil' ass up out of here. You can finish playing later."

He jumped down and stomped out of the room slamming the door behind himself.

"I don't never have problems with my two lil' girls, but that lil' nigga there? He gon' be just like me, I can see it now."

Quay nodded his head in agreement. "I remember when that nigga was born. I had just caught my first body and got my first baby mamma pregnant. That was one helluva year," he said while reflecting on the time period six years ago.

"I know right. Time flying like a muthafucka. Wassup, though?" Black asked after adjusting himself in the bed with a slight grimace. He was healing quickly, but there was still pain.

"Just came to check up on you. I heard Big Keisha requested to get you whacked. Wassup with that?" asked Quay.

Black took a deep breath, and shook his head rapidly, trying to shake the bizarre incident out of his head. "The *only* reason she still alive is because of my sister. I don't know what got into her bro, she just spazzed out."

"Why, though?" asked Quay.

"Because I ain't go to G-Baby's funeral. Everybody knows we don't do funerals in this hood," Black admitted sourly.

"Damn, my mamma asked about you, too. She told me to give you her blessings when I came and saw you," Quay informed trying to cheer him up.

Black nodded his head. "What's new out there in them streets though? All I been hearing is what Clara been hearing from the Dinero Girls, and you know how they do."

"Them girls so damn extra. A nigga can hit a lick for five-gees, two pounds, and shoot a nigga in the ass, and they gon' tell everybody he hit for one-hundred gees, fifteen brick of Heroin, and killed three niggas!" Quay stated jokingly.

They both laughed at the joke.

"You making my ribs hurt, nigga," Black said while holding his side, but he couldn't deny the fact that it felt good to have a good laugh. He hadn't been doing too much of that lately.

"My bad, bro'. But on some real shit, it's real out there in them streets. The lil' nigga Mooski got into a shootout with some niggas on the Southside while scoping out a move, and accidentally shot a six-year-old lil' girl in the head. Now the Dinero Guys out that way at war with them niggas," Quay stated intensely.

Black's eyes got big.

"You know Maniac had got banned from the city for that shit he did. All he had to do was stay out of Atlanta, but you know him, he gon' break the rules just because he can. So, of course, he came back out here. The nigga just pulled back up in the hood like shit all good. Toe-Tag ain't put up too much of a fuss about it because that's Maniac, but guess what? That nigga Kapo got word, and you know he on the *bullshit* these days. So, he made Toe-Tag whack Maniac himself, and record it for him," said Quay.

Black's eyes got bigger and his jaw dropped.

"I know you been hearing about how the police been killing and beating niggas. We damn near at war with them folks. They don't like Crips, Bloods, or GDs, but them fuck niggas *hate* us! They trying to do us like BMF bro'. The only time we might live through a traffic stop is in the daytime, or in public where it's a lot of people, and cameras. But if we cross paths in the backstreets, or anywhere where it's not a lot of witnesses around, we either take 'em on a high-speed chase, or we just start shooting. So, Kapo made it mandatory that we ride deep everywhere," said Quay.

This was too much for Black. How the hell was all this going on without him knowing. He'd just realized how isolated he'd been from the camp. "How the fuck did shit get this bad, that fast?"

Quay shrugged his shoulders. "I don't know, but I do know this—it's gon' get worse."

***

The gambling house in Eagle Run was jumping seven days a week. Males, and females, from the age of twelve on up. If you had money, you could come in, and try your luck.

Monster was participating in a game of spades enjoying the little downtime he did have. Niggas like him did too much dirt in the streets to be going out regularly like a regular nigga. That's why he and Toe-Tag were encouraging the Mobsters in their camp to go out as less as possible and stay in the shadows.

He had ZyAsia on his team playing against an old couple from the hood when Dead Shot walked up to the table asking to talk to him in private. They'd been seeing a lot of each other lately. Toe-Tag had fallen back, so he could play his role correctly, and left the physical aspect to Monster.

At first, Monster didn't like him just because he used to run behind Vonte, but after they did a few jobs together, and took a few souls together, they formed some kind of bond.

He made Dead Shot wait until the game was over because he had a $750 bet on it. After they won, he gave the winnings, to ZyAsia, and told her to go back to the apartment. He knew he wouldn't be returning to the gambling house.

Once they were in the back of Dead Shot's Escalade, Monster, fired up a cigarette. "What's going on?" he asked ready to hear the bad news.

Dead Shot shook his head with his big lips pursed together displaying a very serious face. "The good part is, I just had to whack two of mine because they were snitching. The bad part is, I don't know how long they been snitching, or how much they told."

That caught Monster's attention. "Who?"

Dead Shot told him, "The *same* two niggas we took with us on the Dunwoody job?"

Monster growled in irritation. "Damnnn, shawty!" he spat while punching the back of the driver's seat making the shooter that sat in it bounce forward abruptly. "They must've been paying them niggas, or something?"

"Hell no. They got caught up with some guns and saved themselves. They wasn't working for the police either," Dead Shot informed.

"I'm at the point where I don't even give a fuck no more. I bet you I go out like a G if it come down to it," Monster promised.

Dead Shot waved him off. "Just chill, they'll come for me before they come for you. So, if you get caught that's your fault."

"I ain't doing no running!" Monster barked stubbornly.

"Like I said, it'll be your fault. I'm about to head across town to go check on that lil' package, so I can make it back before the sun go down. I ain't got time to be playing cops and robbers tonight," Dead Shot informed matter-a-factly.

Monster dapped him up. "Alright. Hit me up on the Trac phone and keep me posted."

"I was gon' break the news to you over the phone, but thought you was gon' want to hear that face-to-face."

"You thought right," Monster said before hopping out of the truck.

***

Dead Shot's right-hand man, Odee, woke him up out of his seat with a push to the shoulder.

He grabbed Odee's hand with a death-grip. "What?"

"Wake up, man. We here," Odee informed as he snatched his hand away from him. "You driving back to the hood, and I'm sleeping next time."

"Yeah, right."

Dead Shot got out of the car. "Agggghhh!" he yelled out as he took a long stretch.

They were in the back yard of a drug-house right off Old National Boulevard that Dead Shot's cousin, Reno operated out of. It was a clean and quiet spot due to the fact that his cousin only used it to package, and store weed. So, he paid him to use it for a temporary holding cell for his hostage's.

He and Monster had been up to *a lot* lately. They had Stacy snatched up since her father wanted to orchestrate a fake kidnapping, so they took it upon themselves to show him what the real deal felt like. He was currently scrambling to get the million dollars in cash together for them.

The manhunt for Vonte was starting to become cold. It's like the nigga fell off the face of the earth. Toe-Tag found out about, Violence, and how close she was to Vonte. So, he sent them to snatch her up. Unlike Stacy, she wasn't labeled untouched. They had Mobsters torturing her for Vonte's location, but they were starting to believe that she really didn't know where he was. That, or she just loved the nigga that much.

Dead Shot zipped his Ralph Lauren coat up and instructed the shooters that were in the Yukon behind him to stay in the truck but to keep their eyes open for anything strange.

"Want me to come in with you?" Odee asked expectantly. He was older than Dead Shot by a few years, but their personalities were vice versa. He was a big, goofy-looking nigga with a beer belly, that loved gunplay and following orders. Prime reason why Dead Shot kept him around. He was one of the most loyal niggas you'd ever meet. "Yeah, I'm gon' need somebody with me."

He saw Reno's white Dodge Challenger on the curb. So, he knew he was there, but he didn't know if anybody else was there. He barely trusted his cousin, so you know he didn't trust another nigga.

He tried calling Reno's phone, but it rang out all the way to the voicemail three times. He started knocking on the door, he could hear the music playing inside. He tried the knob, but the door was locked.

"Aye run around front real quick and see if the front door's unlocked," he instructed Odee while trying to call Reno again.

Odee came back with bad news, so he did the next logical thing and broke in. He broke the glass in the square closest to the doorknob and let himself in like that.

Reno kept the weed in the basement, and the rest of the house was basically furniture free, so they kept the girls upstairs in two different rooms with the windows boarded up from the outside, and quadruple locks on the doors. The only two people with keys to the locks were Dead Shot and Reno. The only reason Reno had a pair was just in case of an emergency if he needed to clear the spot out.

They neared Stacy's room first, so he unlocked the door and checked on her. He was about to open the door until Odee stopped him. "You ain't got nothing over your face!" he whispered urgently.

"Damn, I'm tripping." He pulled the black bandana out of his back pocket and wrapped it around his face covering it from the eyes down.

He opened the door and stuck his head in. Stacy was laying on the single mattress on the floor watching *How High* on the TV that he put in there for her. She looked bored and scared.

"You hungry?" he asked as he stuck his head in.

She just looked at him with her pink hair wearing the same grey, Juicy Couture sweatsuit that she had on two days ago when they snatched her up.

"Another man just fed me," she answered while pointing at an empty Subway bag. "Did my daddy pay you, yet? This is the second time I've got kidnapped in a month. I can't take it anymore. I'm surprised he still has money left. I know it won't be a third time because he's definitely going to be broke after this."

"Just be glad you not in the same position as the other hoe down the hall," he suggested before closing the door back and securing the locks.

They walked down towards the master bedroom on the end where Violence was being held. Her set up was a lot less comfortable than Stacy's. Plastic covered the floor and the walls, and she was tied up butt naked with tape covering her mouth.

She was one tuff cookie because he'd had a lot of niggas fold before her. That's the main reason he was starting to believe she really didn't know where Vonte was.

The only piece of furniture was a portable stereo that you could hook up to a phone and play music off. It was used to drown out the sound of her screams when she was being tortured, but the only people allowed to do that was Dead Shot's men. So, there was no reason why the music should be playing, or the door should've been ajar.

He walked into the room and was frozen by the horrific scene. He'd seen a lot of shit in his life, but he never saw anything quite like this. Violence's right leg was literally four times its normal size, and it was purplish. He could see it good because Reno's fat ass was holding her leg's in the air while he laid in between them and pumped away at her limp body.

He couldn't take the scene anymore, so he looked at Reno and nodded his head towards them. Odee nodded his head, stalked up behind Reno, who was still oblivious to their presence and put him in a chokehold pulling him up onto his feet. He started fidgeting like a fish and grabbing at Odee's arm trying to get free.

"Please tell me what the *fuck* you got goin' on!" Dead Shot commanded after unplugging the phone from the stereo.

He was trying to talk, but Odee prevented him from doing so. "How the fuck he supposed to answer me if you choking the life out the nigga?"

"My bad," Odee said before letting him go.

"Sh-she—dead! A spider bit her on the leg or some shit. She was like that when I saw her," he answered heavily still out of breath.

Dead Shot waved him off. "I can see that, but what I'm trying to figure out is why you in here fucking a dead bitch, Reno? What you think yo' mamma gon' think if she heard about this shit? You getting plenty of money/ I know you can't be hurting for no pussy like that, man."

Tears started welling up in his eyes. "I've been following this bitch for the longest on Instagram, and wanted to fuck her so bad, but she wouldn't budge for shit! So, when you brought her here it was like it was meant to be. I fucked her for the first time yesterday and came back for seconds today because I ain't know when you was gon' have her killed. The bitch was already dead with her leg looking like this. I just figured I'd hit her for the last time since it didn't look like she was dead for that long."

Dead Shot and Odee looked at each other in confusion trying desperately to understand where he was coming from, but they just couldn't. "I never knew you was sick like this, Reno. It's crazy how you can know somebody yo' whole life, and not know them at all. Since you want to lay up with the bitch, you gon' be the one to get rid of the body. Yo' stupid ass lucky the condom ain't pop. She's full of poison dumb-ass-nigga!"

"Don't look at me different, cuz. That ain't me, I just fucked up."

Dead Shot waved him off dismissively. "Whatever. Just know if you touch that little teenage girl in that other room, I'm gon' make you eat a Viagra, and stick an icepick down yo dick you sick muthafucka," he promised before storming out of the room dialing Monster's number to let him know about Violence.

Odee looked him up-and-down unimpressively. "He ain't mean to say icepick, we gon' have to stick a Q-tip down that lil' shit!" he said laughing at his own joke.

CHAPTER 13

Kapo had just finished another meeting with his acquisition team in the same Midtown office he'd been renting. He had an office in his house, but he couldn't have too much company over there, plus he needed a professional office in the city.

This time, instead of his business lawyer returning after the meeting, it was, Ms. Sung the financial advisor. Well, she really never left the office, she just hung behind.

"Can I speak with you in private, Mr. Cooper?"

"You can call me, Kapo. And we are in the office alone, right? Wassup? Talk to me," he said then stated.

She walked back towards his desk. "I'm not going to lie, I've been following up on you, and everything you have going on. Did you know there are over twenty articles about you on the internet?"

"I knew there was some, but not that many. What you getting at, though?"

She took a deep breath trying to control her anxiety. His powerful aura was suffocating her even though the office was very spacious and well ventilated. "I'm just amazed by the fact that you're up and running after everything you've been, and still are going through. The average man would've put a bullet in his head."

He kept his predatory eyes focused on hers trying to look past her into her soul. He stood up, walked around his desk, and closed the distance between them. "Do I look like a regular nigga to you?"

She was 5'1, so she had to look all the way up at him while he was standing that close. She was in a wonderful place in between being intimidated and aroused. "No, you are every bit of the powerful figure they've made you out to be."

"Strip," he demanded simply.

She took a defensive step back. "Excuse me?"

"You heard me." He scanned her body while undressing her with his eyes. "If you want to stay in this office you need to strip. So, I can check you for a wire, I don't trust nobody."

A big part of her told her to walk out of the office, but a small part of her told her to submit to his command, and that small part was very powerful at the moment. She wore a white blouse with a black dress skirt that stopped right above her knees. She put her hands behind her back and unzipped her skirt.

Thirty seconds later, she stood awkwardly in front of him in her lingerie. "You happy now?"

He shook his head with his eyes on the wonderful gap in between her legs. "No, I got to pat you down."

He started down at her ankles and ran his big hands up her thighs slowly enjoying the feel of her smooth skin. It's been a month since he'd even thought about sex, and she was bringing it up out of him. His dick was rock hard, and he didn't even make it up to the plump piece of fruit in between her legs yet.

When he did make it there, she gasped audibly, and his dick surprisingly got harder. "You dripping through your panties, baby girl. Am I turning you on?" he asked while caressing her pussy through the silky fabric of her panties.

"What are you doing to me?"

He stood all the way up with his hand still palming her pussy and leaned in for a sloppy kiss. She was overwhelmed by the experience. It's been over a year since she'd been physical with a man. Her career, and family, had been her life up until now.

He wrapped both of his hands behind her back and slid them down to her ass. She had a round healthy apple bottom, unlike most Asian women. He gripped it and picked her up. She wrapped both legs around his waist out of reflex.

He loved how light she felt in his arms. He pulled his pants down enough to get his dick out, shoved her panties to the side, and rammed himself inside her dripping wet love-nest.

"Ahhh-owww, it's so big!" she cried out in pain and bliss. She'd been fantasizing about a black dick inside of her since she was a teenager.

He started off slow so she could get used to the feeling of him digging into her guts. After she came on his dick twice, he sped it up.

"It's my turn," he grunted while pounding away.

The sound of their skin clapping together rapidly sounded like a round of applause. He released a month's worth of cum into her, then leaned back onto the desk for support because he had suddenly become weak. Her legs was stretched out on the desk and her arms was still wrapped around his neck, so she wouldn't fall. "That was literally the best experience I've witness in my life."

"That was just the warmup," he informed matter-a-factly sporting a smug smirk.

She took a deep breath again her anxiety was back.

"Boss, there's an extremely tall man out here requesting to see you," Glock informed with his head stuck inside the door.

Ms. Sue was caught off guard and made the mistake of unclasping her hands from around his neck for a second, and that's all it took for her to take that fall to the ground.

Kapo pulled his pants up while she crawled over to her clothes, so she could put them on.

"What's his name?" he asked irritably.

"He never gave an exact name. All he said was that he's the Godfather of most Godfathers, something like that."

***

2-Tall walked into the office as Ms. Sue was walking out. He looked down at her with interest and let his eyes follow her as she walked out of the office. "Nice—I've been meaning to take this trip for a week now, but I've been tied up with more pressing issues."

Kapo was seated back behind his desk looking up at the man who stood before him. A visit from him could mean only two things. Extraordinary life, or guaranteed death. He had more legends told about him than Dinero himself.

"You just gon' sit there staring at me, or you gon' invite me to a seat?"

"Invite yourself to a seat. You do everything else you want to do."

2-Tall took his advice and sat down after taking his sandy brown Hermes trench coat off and laying it across his legs. "I've been keeping up with you lately, and I'm impressed."

"I've been hearing a lot of that lately."

"You're a busy man, and I'm even busier, so there's no room for foreplay. I'm going to cut to the chase. If nobody else knows how toxic the Georgia camp is, you do. We exist in twenty-nine states in the country. I'm not having the same problems with any of them, it's just y'all." Kapo remained silent, so he continued, "Long story short, y'all are making us look bad, and setting a bad example for other, newer, states. I want to shut y'all out, and terminate the whole camp, but that's not realistic thinking. Truth is, the Georgia camp is the most lucrative camp in Dilluminati, and I need you to clean it up for me."

"You couldn't have been watching me too closely. If you were, you would've already known that I was doing that already."

"I know exactly what you're trying to do. I'm here to let you know that I'll give you Masio's spot if you succeed. His laziness is making it easy for you. Once you gain complete control over this camp and obtain some structure, I'll make you the Godfather."

Kapo pictured himself as the Godfather and thought about all the things he could accomplish. "Say no more."

"It's a deal then." He stood up and put his coat back on over the off-white, Giovanni suit he wore so stylishly. "I'm sorry for the loss of your daughter, too. I would say the same about your wife, but I think you know why I won't. You're a strong man, Kapo. I need more men like you sitting at my Billion Dollar Round Table," he said before strolling out.

Malik D. Rice

CHAPTER 14

Ronte was in Fifty's downtown condo getting some rest before his show tonight. He had a show at club Mansion on the Southside. The whole city was talking about it, and he knew the place would be super-packed. The world was loving him right now, but it was funny because he was at a point in life where he wasn't even loving himself.

"You just got nominated for a Grammy, and rookie of the year. Ain't no muthafuckin' way you supposed to be sitting right there looking like that," Fifty said while looking down at his partner. He had just come from changing in his bedroom upstairs.

Ronte was sitting on the floor with his back to the sofa sipping on a bottle of Sprite that had two Xanax pills dissolved inside. He looked up at Fifty nonchalantly, and back at the screen of his phone without saying a word.

"Then you been wearing all black for the past couple of weeks. Wassup, my nigga? Vonte M.I.A, but the nigga not dead."

Right as he said the last word, there was knocking on the door. Fifty went to go see who it was. More than likely, it was the rest of the entourage that was supposed to meet them there. He opened the door without looking through the peephole and got the shock of a lifetime when he saw who was standing on the other side.

Twenty seconds later, Fifty walked back into the living room with Vonte on his heel's dressing similarly to Ronte with his dreads veiling his face. Ronte look up at Fifty, then past him, and his jaw dropped. "Brooo!" He jumped up spilling the soda on Fifty's expensive rug and closed the distance between them in record speed. "Where the fuck you been?"

Vonte pushed Ronte off him playfully. "I don't even hug my hoes, nigga. Get yo' gay ass up off me."

"Lame ass nigga! You had me worried like a muthafucka. What you gon' do? I tried to get Uncle Freddy to clear yo' name but that nigga talking about he couldn't. So, I hung up on that nigga, and ain't talk to him since."

Vonte shook his head unapprovingly. "Nah, bro, don't be mad at him. It's 'way' over his head. Ain't shit he can do about it, plus it ain't his fault I'm in this situation, but guess what, I'm super straight. Don't worry about me."

Ronte looked behind him and turned around. "Come sit down, bro'. We can kick a lil' shit before my show start. Matter-a-fact, I'll cancel that muthafucka."

"Nah, bro, go do your show. You know my situation, I got to get back to where I'm going."

Ronte couldn't even hide the look of disappointment on his face. "Alright."

"Don't worry lil' nigga. I ain't gon' let these fuck niggas kill me. Keep doing yo' thing out here and making me proud. I'm gon' be in the shadows watching."

"How I'm gon' get in contact with you?"

"I'm gon' pop-up from time to time. You might not know when or where just know I'm coming," he informed before ruffling Ronte's hair roughly and letting himself out the way he came.

***

"Good for her ass," Toe-Tag said after Monster informed him of Violence's accident.

"Guess what else I done heard?"

"What?"

"One of the Monsters that was sent to escort Ronte to his show tonight said they thought they saw Vonte in a Yukon that was driving away from the condos as they pulled up."

Toe-Tag nodded his head. "I can go for that. If he don't care about nobody else, he care about, Ronte. I'll kidnap that nigga to draw Vonte out if I thought I could get away with it."

"You crazy," Monster said as he saw a group of Armenians walking up to their truck from the small warehouse. "There they go."

Toe-Tag instructed Valencia to stay in the truck and drive off if she heard gunshots. He hopped out the back of the truck with Monster. Monster carried his fully equipped AR-15 with three clips, and Toe-Tag carried a small duffle bag filled with blue hundreds.

"The boss will see you now," a well-built man, that looked like a strong believer in steroids, informed in a heavy Armenian accent.

They were escorted inside the warehouse, and it was nothing either one of them would've expected. A dozen colorful foreign cars were lined up horizontally in two rows of six. There were plush white leather sofas here and there. A black marble granite dancefloor in the middle of the cars. Stripper poles on mini stages here and there, along with two bars, and four pool tables.

"Damn," was all Toe-Tag could say.

An insanely good-looking man came walking down a flight of wraparound stairs. He was draped in a white tailor-made Saint Laurent suit. His shoulder-length dirty blonde hair was lightly jelled back in sophisticated style, and his dark grey eyes were locked onto them.

His name was, Gilmore, and he currently ran the Armenian Mafia in Georgia. They made their fortune from human-trafficking, and gun-trafficking. The only reason he was even doing business with Toe-Tag is because he informed him that he was the one that took out his completion, Xavier. For that, he was grateful and embraced him.

"Dinero Guys. How are you tonight?" he asked with just a hint of an accent as he walked up to them.

"I've had worst, this is a nice place you got here. I wasn't expecting it to look like this from the outside."

He smiled at Toe-Tag, he loved when people complimented his place. "I've spent over ten-million dollars on this place. Decorating it is a hobby for me these days."

Toe-Tag took another look around. "I see."

"Come, I know how you Dinero Guys are. Like to get straight to the business, right? Follow me."

He led them toward the staircase, and that's when Toe-Tag realized that it didn't end on the ground level. It kept going underground. Gilmore led the way down the stairs, and everybody else followed.

"That was my lobby, and *this*, this is my laboratory," he informed as the narrow staircase opened up to a huge green-lighted room.

"God damn!" Monster blurted as he looked around in gun-heaven.

Gilmore smiled showing his near-perfect teeth. The guy could've easily been a supermodel but chose to follow in his father's footsteps. "That's right, big guy. We have everything from 22. revolvers, to heat-seeking rocket launchers."

Guns of every size were hanging on racks that were lined up in rows throughout the room. It looked like a scene out of the Matrix.

"It's about to be Christmas all over again for my shooters," Toe-Tag stated excitedly. He couldn't wait to let one of the exotic guns rip.

"Pick whatever your money can afford. I'll throw the bullets in at half-price since you complimented my lobby."

Toe-Tag and Monster gave each other a knowing look. The streets of Atlanta were about to get *real* bloody.

Malik D. Rice

CHAPTER 15

It was a warm day for it to be the middle of January. The news forecast said that it was going to be sixty-two degrees, and Black took it as a sign to catch some fresh air. This would be his first time stepping outside of the apartment other than being on the balcony.

Ciara walked in the room and saw him putting on his Gucci jacket. She stopped in her tracks. "Where the hell you going, bae?" she asked curiously. Black's been in the apartment going on two months now, so she was surprised to see him dressing up.

"They said it's supposed to be sixty degrees today. So, I'm about to take Vernon to the basketball court and play with him."

She smiled showing her white teeth that were laced with braces. She was loving him more and more by the day. Since he'd been out of commission, they'd built, and bonded more than they have in the seven years they'd been dealing with each other.

"You sure you healed up enough to be out there running around with him?"

He leaned back as far as he could go, side to side, then slowly stretched his hands down and touched his toes. "I ain't gon' be able to dunk, so I'll just shoot a bunch of threes," he stated jokingly.

She rushed into the closet.

"What you doing?"

"Getting dressed, nigga, I'm coming too."

Black went out on the basketball court and played with his little man. He was careful not to do too much to hurt himself, but for the most part, he'd healed nicely.

First, a few Dinero Girls came to kick it with Ciara because they hadn't been seeing too much of her either. Then, a few kids around the neighborhood came on the court and started playing with Vernon, so Black took a break, and just started watching them. After that, Mobsters started pulling up to kick it with Black. An old head pulled out his grill, and it turned into a whole BBQ out of nowhere.

It didn't take long for Toe-Tag, and Monster to pop-up on the scene. He received mad love from everybody. He was the man of the year. He found Black quickly and walked straight up to him. By this time, he was sitting on the bench drinking a Pepsi with Ciara on his lap.

"Black, wassup, nigga? I thought you would never come up out that damn apartment," Toe-Tag said as he walked up with Monster on his heels.

Black told Ciara to get up and let him talk to Toe-Tag. "I had to get back right. I'm a Mafioso, can't have folks seeing me like that." He said after dapping both of them up.

Toe-Tag took a seat on the bench next to him, and Monster remained standing. "I feel you. Take as much time as you need to get right. Physically, and mentally. I got work for you soon as you're able to do it. All the Mafiosos in the camp got their own kill-teams now, so you gon' have to pick you some Mobsters to keep with you."

"Aight, I heard shit been off the chain out here, too."

Toe-Tag leaned back on the bench with his legs stretched out. He scanned the block and looked around at all the people that he was responsible for. "You don't even know the half of what a young nigga been going through, shawty."

"I can only imagine. You holding that shit down and handling your business. Just got to slow down on the bodies."

Toe-Tag looked at him with a raised brow. "What?"

"You heard me, bro'. A lot of the blood that's being shed in our name be unnecessary. Look at the example we're painting for the Baby Mobsters. They're only goal is to grow up being better than us which is really worse than us. Look at, Mooski," he said while pointing at the young Mafioso who was showing off a fully-automatic handgun with a fifty-round drum to a group of Baby Mobsters. "That lil' nigga like a new-born vampire. He out of control."

"Where all this shit coming from? Don't tell me you done turned into Malcolm X in that hospital bed?" Toe-Tag joked. "We eat off murder. That ain't nothing new out here. If one of them Baby Mobsters catch a body right now, I ain't gon' get mad at 'em, and give 'em a lecture. I'm gon' give 'em a DG chain. You know why? Because it's in them."

Black put his hands up in surrender. "I'm just a small-fry. I was just saying. But you know them same nightmares you be having at night? That distant feeling you feel when you lookin' in the mirror at a stranger? Is that what you want for them? Because I don't want that shit for my son, shawty. Think about yo' son. Just because they from the hood, don't mean they got to be killers. A lot of these young niggas got other talents than squeezing triggers. Look at, AK," he said before getting up off the bench and walking away.

Malik D. Rice

CHAPTER 16

Pablo was at one of his stash houses watching a group of Dinero Girls count his money for him. He was having so much of the shit these days that it was getting harder and harder to keep count of the shit. He had to make a mental note to hire him an accountant.

His phone rang, and he picked it up even though he didn't recognize the number. "Yo."

"This Pablo, right?"

"Yeah. Who is this?"

"This, Wopp."

Pablo took the phone away from his ear and looked at it. Woppp was the Underboss over Dilluminati for the Southside of Atlanta. He'd never talked to Wopp a day in his life, but all the Underbosses in the city made it a point to know of each other.

He thought about asking him how he got his number, but more than likely he'd got it from Freddy. Plus, there was a question he wanted to ask more. "What you need?"

"I need to get some understanding because me and you got a problem."

Pablo clenched his teeth and ran his free hand through his dreads in frustration. He knew about Mooski's situation and had been hearing about the escalating war between the Gotti Gang niggas, and the Dinero Guys on the Southside. That's why he wasn't really surprised to hear from Wopp, he'd been waiting on a visit, or call. "I ain't got shit to do with that."

He heard Wopp laugh amusingly. "You know why Dinero locked up right now? Not because of all the shit he did, but because of all the shit, Dilluminati was doing. The downside about being a leader is that you're responsible for the shit that your followers do."

"I get it. What you want me to do?"

"Set me up a sit down with the young nigga that came in my hood like a lonely cowboy. I want to look him in his eyes when I talk to him."

"When?"

"I'm on the way to your neck of the woods now. I say about thirty minutes."

"A'ight, I'm about to call his Don now because I'm not in the city right now."

Forty-five minutes later, a white Lamborghini with black tinted windows and black rims pulled up into Eagle Run followed by a black Yukon. He was told to park in front of the building in the back where a bunch of niggas was posted up, just like Toe-Tag said, he couldn't miss it.

He parked in the middle of the street and hopped out of the car. After instructing his kill-team to stay put, he walked toward the apartment building. One of the Mobsters told him what apartment Toe-Tag was in, and he proceeded, he knocked on apartment 2C.

A big, light-skinned nigga with a beard opened the door. He knew it wasn't Toe-Tag because he'd looked the young nigga up on Instagram while he was on his way there, but he did remember the face from the page. "You must be, Monster?"

Monster nodded and stepped to the side so he could walk inside. Toe-Tag sat on the couch with his feet on the coffee table next to three large stacks of money. Mooski sat on the other couch clutching an AR-15 stalking Wopp like prey, and Monster took a spot on the wall standing.

"What's good?"

Toe-Tag looked up at Wopp observantly. He tried to look him up on Instagram as well, but Wopp wasn't a big fan of social media. He didn't want a nigga laying on him like he just did Toe-Tag.

He would've never thought Wopp was so small. Well, he wasn't all that small. He was 185 pounds standing at 5'8, but his voice didn't match his size. He had a deep, booming voice that would make you think he was Monster's size. You could tell he had a little age on him by his skin and the fact that his hairline was receding tremendously.

Monster grabbed a foldable chair and place it behind Wopp, and he sat down.

"You tell me, you're the one that called this meeting."

"I know you know about the issues I been having on my side of town because of this lil' nigga right here? I came all the way out this way to get some understanding."

Toe-Tag squinted his eyes suspiciously. "The way Pablo put it was like you was trying to pull up for some straightening."

"We already handled our business on the Southside, and the beef is squashed between us, and Gotti Gang. However, I think this lil' nigga need to suffer some type of consequences for his reckless actions," he said before cutting his eyes at, Mooski, who was glaring at him grimly.

Toe-Tag laughed in his face. "Consequences?" He looked over at Mooski. "Tell him what happened."

Mooski sat up straight on the couch. "I was on the way back to the hood to report to Toe-Tag, but I had to stop at a gas station. When I was at the gas station a group of hoes called me from some apartments that's on the side of the gas station, so I pumped my gas and pulled up over there. I was chopping it up with the hoes when one of their boyfriends came over trying to check me 'bout a bitch I wasn't even talking to. I was talking to her friend. I tried to tell the stupid ass nigga that, but he tried to flex his lil' muscles in front of them hoes thinking I was gon' fold. So, I let it rip on them fuck niggas, end of story."

Toe-Tag smiled sarcastically. "What he said—end of story."

"No, that ain't the end of the story. One of them niggas got whacked, two niggas got shot, one of them girls got shot, and last but *definitely* not least you shot a lil' girl in the head! You must've been shooting with yo' eyes closed?" he asked aggressively.

"My eyes wide open right now! Fuck you mean?" Mooski barked back with his grip getting tighter on the AR.

Toe-Tag motioned with his hands telling Mooski to pipe down. "Look, I ain't saying fuck the lil' girl's life, but you been in the game longer than me. You know how this shit go. Sometimes it's gon' be casualties, it happens."

"Okay, well how about this. We had mob-ties with Gotti Gang. Now that's out the window. How you would you have felt if it was the other way around, and one of my shooters came out here and flipped PDE?"

"He wouldn't have made it out that muthafucka. That's the difference," Toe-Tag replied jokingly making Monster laugh as well.

Wopp looked around the room, in disgust. He had to take a deep breath to keep himself from saying something that would probably prevent him from making it out of there. "Then what? Y'all still would've been at war with them, and the mob-ties would've been cut."

"Probably so, but that's not what happened, so it's irrelevant."

"Look, I ain't telling you to whack the young nigga. At least ban him from the city or some shit. Something got to happen."

Toe-Tag sat straight up and looked Wopp dead in the eyes. He did his homework on him and knew he wasn't a bitch, but he also knew he wasn't ready for the type of problems that he could bring his way. Everybody knew the Eastside camp had most of the muscle when it came to Dilluminati.

"This what's gone happen—you gon' get in yo' car, drive back to the Southside, go home, grab a piece of chalk, and mark you a line on that chalkboard because ain't shit like that going on."

Wopp mugged him and sat there for a second trying to choose his next words carefully. He couldn't do anything at the moment, so he'd lost the battle, but Toe-Tag had officially made his shit list. He was one who knew how to hold a grudge. "Okay, big dawg. I appreciate your time." He got up and let himself out.

When he was gone Toe-Tag, Monster, and Mooski all looked at each other seriously until Toe-Tag's laughter started spilling out. "What if shit was the other way around? Stop it! Them niggas *know* they ain't built like that for real. Probably got like ten real shooters in that whole camp."

"I'm trying to tell you," Mooski said. "'Preciate you for havin' my back, bro'."

Toe-Tag threw up their hand sign and wiggled it slightly. If you were to hold up five fingers with the palm facing you and drop the finger in between your index finger, and ring finger, you'd be throwing it up. The index finger and the thumb made up the *L*, the four remaining fingers made up the *4*, and the index finger, ring finger, and pinky, made up the *E*.

"Loyalty 4 Eva, nigga. That's that shit I stand on."

Malik D. Rice

CHAPTER 17

Handsome sat on his bed counting the last little bit of the $40,000 he had laying on top of it.

"You don't think that's a little too much? I don't think I'm worth all that," Kamya said from beside him.

He looked at her in the cute, little, purple Burberry skirt-shirt, black leggings, and shoes to match the skirt, that he'd bought her. "You're worth way-way more than this beautiful, but it's not just about you. It's about my soul, too. I need it back." He pulled her in for a long kiss, stuffed the money in his bookbag, and left her in the apartment with her own anxiety.

Monster answered Toe-Tag's door and let him in. He walked in and saw Mooski on one couch sleep, cuddled up with his gun, and Toe-Tag was on video chat with Shanay.

"Aye, can I talk to you in the back real quick?"

Toe-Tag looked up at him irritably. "Come on, man. You know how long it took her to answer the phone for me?"

"This shit important, bro'. It ain't gon' take long, though."

He told Shanay he would call her back and took Handsome to his bedroom. "Wassup?" he asked after taking a seat on his bed.

Handsome took the Nike book bag off and tossed it at him.

"What's this for? You just hit a lick, or some shit?" he asked while holding a stack of the twenties in his hand.

"Nah, you know my cousin be doing his lil' thang with the scams, and shit. He a Mafioso in Papa's camp and offered me a spot on his money-team."

You would've thought Toe-Tag drunk a swallow of spoiled milk by the way he twisted his face up. "What you saying? You tryin' to jump camps?" He couldn't hide the shock, and disappointment in his voice even if he wanted to. He took pride in all his Mafiosos.

"Just hear me out first before you go to acting crazy, and shit. I'm in love with, Kamya, dawg. Like I knew her my whole life, but in the last month we done really got to know each other and became soulmates. I'm tryin' to start a family with her, and not have her up at night worrying herself wondering if I'm gon' make it home, or not. I want to know I'm gon' be able to watch my kids grow up. You know firsthand how much work I done put in for the hood. I done did missions for you, that only me, and you, know about. I'm just asking you for a pass. I want my soul back, bro'. Take that $40,000 right there, and I'm gon' pay you $40,000 every month for four months after this, then my debts will be paid."

Toe-Tag reflected on what he said for a minute. He did put in a lot of work, and he'd always been there whenever he was called upon. He stayed Loyal 4, Eva, through it all, but he got involved with Kamya and was really trying to do right by her. How could he get in the way of that? Especially when he knew Rampage was probably looking up at him right now trying to see what he was going to say.

"You chose the right bitch, boy. 'Cause if you would've told me you was tryin' to jump camps for *any* other bitch I would've spazzed-out, but I want to see Kamya happy, she deserves that. Make sure you do right by her, nigga."

Handsome looked at him suspiciously. "Sooo, you really gon' let me out?"

"Yeah, nigga!" he answered playfully. "Everybody in the hood gon' call you soft, but that's on you."

"Fuck them, niggas! They know wassup with me. They'll understand once they got enough of this shit."

Toe-Tag understood where Handsome was coming from. He really envied Handsome because he wished someone could do that for him, but that was out of the question. He had too many people depending on him. "Just pay me my money, nigga, and enjoy your life out there. Go see the world and make that girl happy. Make sure you stay in touch, too."

Handsome smiled happily. This was the first time he felt hope in a *long* time. It's like a small piece of his soul was restored already. Kamya, and the kids they planned on having, were going to restore the rest. It's been a long time since he talked to God, but he thanked him at that moment, and he thanked his friend. "Thank you, man. I'm gon' make her the happiest woman on earth," he vowed seriously.

"Get out my spot lovey-dovey ass nigga! Go pack yo' shit. You need to be out of the hood by sunrise. I'm 'bout to call Shanay back and tell her what I just did for yo' ass, so I can get me some pussy," he joked before embracing his brother.

Malik D. Rice

CHAPTER 18

"You honestly think you can tame those animals? You know that we have over a dozen lawmen in the metro Atlanta area that are going to counseling for some of the crime scenes your boys have left behind? Do you know how many grieving family members are calling my office screaming for justice? That's why I told my boys to target yours," Sheriff McFarland stated seriously.

He was the sheriff over DeKalb county and he wanted this nightmare to end just as much as Kapo did. He was a redneck who'd grown up in the outskirts of Decatur, Georgia.

Kapo had reached out to him and offered $25,000 just for a private sit-down. Of course, he showed up, and now there they were. Two generals on different sides of the field coming together trying to end a war.

"Listen, I know you don't agree with our way of living, and our reasons for doing things, but the *D* in Dilluminati doesn't stand for destruction. We do a lot of good, too, but nobody wants to acknowledge that part, though."

"We're not targeting Dilluminati as a whole. We just want Toe-Tag and his boys at this point. Vonte was the main focus, but since he's vanished off the face of the earth, all fingers are pointing at him. We have reason to believe he and his boys are responsible for at least sixty percent of the murder rate, and that's a big problem. You ever heard of the old saying, *bodies bring heat*? It just so happens to be true. You think I like the FBI snooping all around my backyard? No, I don't."

Kapo wanted to sigh heavily and put his face in his hands. He was going through so much, mentally that it was wearing him down, but he had to keep going even though he'd lost everything. He'd never been a quitter, and something just told him to keep going, so that's what he was doing.

"We both know murder in our city can't be stopped, but what if I can slow it down?"

"You'd be doing the community a great service. I could get my boys to play fair ball with you guys, but I can't control the federal government, though."

Kapo nodded understandably. "We've been dealing with the feds, it's cool, but the heat we've been receiving from your boys is the more immediate problem. I'm losing a lot of money."

"I just want that murder rate dropped, so I can look productive to the mayor."

"Cool, there you go. Just a little compensation for the *community*." He slid a brown paper bag across the table. It was twice the amount of money he paid for the sit-down.

McFarland took a peep inside and licked his lips that had suddenly become chap. "Thank you for your contribution. I'll be in touch," he informed knowingly before getting up and exiting the office.

When he left, Kapo spun his chair around to face the wall-length window that overlooked a good portion of the city. He was still amazed at how effective you could be with the almighty dollar.

***

Masio, and Freddy, had a sit down at Bizzy's every other Friday. They made it a point to stay in tune with each other.

"Where the hell yo' glasses at, man?" Freddy asked, Masio after he got finished flirting with a thick Brazilian waitress who he'd been fucking lately.

Masio gave him an awkward look. "I wear shades nigga, not glasses."

"Nah, nigga. I don't mean literally. I'm saying like, you can't see what's goin' on?"

"What the hell you talkin' about, Freddy?" he asked before taking a bite out of his shrimp salad.

"That nigga, Kapo. He trying to take yo' spot. He doing too much."

Masio chucked amusingly.

"You think that shit funny?"

"Nah, I think it's true. That's why I'm laughing. You know I don't give a fuck about this Godfather shit. That's what I want him to do."

"If 2-Tall decides to replace you with him. What you think he gon' do with you?"

"Bump me back down to the Pope."

Freddy made a knowing face. "You better hope yo' ass don't end up like, Drop Top."

Masio's smug look disappeared.

Malik D. Rice

CHAPTER 19

Toe-Tag was laying in the bed watching TV until the TV eventually started watching him. The cocaine had him up for four days straight, and he was just now getting to winding down. He could stay in the bed for days if he wanted because he knew the Mafiosos would handle whatever needed to be handled and wouldn't bother him unless it was absolutely necessary. He'd been sleeping peacefully for all of three hours when his phone rang. At first, he thought he was dreaming, but after a while, he woke up. By the time he got ready to roll over and grab the phone, it stopped ringing. As soon as he closed his eyes again it started ringing again.

He rolled over, grabbed the phone and swiped it without looking at the caller I.D. "Who done died now, man?" he asked groggily with enough aggravation thrown in to split between two people.

"Ain't nobody died. Get yo' ass up. Kapo just called a mandatory meeting for all the made-men in my camp," Pablo informed urgently.

He sucked his diamond teeth. "Mannn! Tell that nigga to sit his ass down somewhere, shawty," he spat before hanging up the phone and rolling back over.

Five seconds later, the phone rang again. "Aggghhh-fffuckkk!" he growled before picking the phone back up. "Pablo, fuck you and fuck Kapo. Tell that nigga you gon' fill me in 'cause I got the flu or some shit. Be creative." He hung up again, but this time he cut the phone off and tossed it onto the carpeted floor.

Toe-Tag was dreaming about one of his middle school girlfriends for some reason. He had just persuaded her to take off her pants so he and Rampage could run a train on her when gunshots started ringing out and he woke up. It was then that he noticed it wasn't gunshots that interrupted his dream, it was somebody beating on the muthafucking door.

Everybody in his camp knew not to disturb him unless a body dropped, so he knew it wasn't one of his. The only person that came to his mind was, Pablo. He popped up out of his bed, grabbed his fully automatic Glock 18, and stormed to the front door.

He opened it with plans on slapping Pablo across the head with it, but the first face he saw didn't belong to Pablo. It was Kapo's ugly ass, with Pablo and the other three Dons behind him.

"Thought I'd bring the meeting to you since you so sick," Kapo informed sarcastically before inviting himself into the apartment.

They all settled in the living room and listened to what Kapo had to say so badly. Everybody else sat down while he stood. "There's approximately four-hundred and seventy-nine Dinero Guys in our city, and one-hundred and eighty-eight in this camp. That makes y'all the biggest, and basically the most important."

He took his fox fur, mink coat off and laid it on one of the stools that were pulled up to the counter connected to the kitchen. "I just had a talk with the sheriff personally, and I got him on the payroll. He'll make his officers stop harassing us. All we got to do is keep the murder rate down," he said while looking straight at Toe-Tag.

Toe-Tag's face twisted up something serious. "Come on with all this indirect ass shit! You ain't have to call no whole meeting for that. Ain't nobody else in this room droppin' bodies, but *me*! All you had to do was pull up on me one-on-one. Matter-of-fact, y'all niggas get out. Let me chop it up with, Kapo."

Nobody moved, they just looked up at Kapo for assurance.

"Man, I know y'all *fuck niggas* heard me! Get the fuck out before I tear this bitch up!" he blared savagely after standing up startling everyone in the room.

They acted like they heard him this time and left the apartment.

"Look, I ain't in the mood for the bullshit right now. Say what you got to say, so you can go on about your business," he told Kapo seriously before taking his seat on the couch again.

Kapo breathed in and out deeply. "All the bodies y'all leaving around town bringing a lot of heat on us, and the whole Dilluminati suffering for it. This ain't *Grand Theft Auto* where you can go to war with the police, and shit be alright afterward. It's a war we *can't* win. They gon' fall back, all you got to do is tell yo' niggas to sit they asses down somewhere."

"It wasn't no problem when you needed who you needed whacked, though. This is business for me, nigga."

"Just chill, I'm not telling you to stop doing business. I'm just telling you to do it outside the city," he compromised.

Toe-Tag poked his bottom lip out slightly and nodded his head slowly. "I think I can arrange that for you, old school. Now get out my spot, so I can go back to sleep."

"You ain't supposed to talk to the Pope like that."

"Kapo, get yo' Kermit The Frog lookin' ass out my spot mannn!"

Kapo laughed lightly, put on his coat, and pulled a thick yellow envelope out filled with hundreds. "You hold up your end of the deal, and there's more where that came from."

Malik D. Rice

CHAPTER 20

Mooski hung upside down in a dark room with very dim lighting. There was this weird scraping sound in the far distance and a heavy leak that sounded like it was coming from a pipe. It was torturous because it was impossibly hot in the room, and he was badly dehydrated.

He tried to pull himself up to undo the restraints on his ankles, but he couldn't bring himself to do it. "Fuck!" he spat irritably.

"It's not going to work, mister," a child's voice called out from a distance, but it sounded closer than the leak.

That was the first voice Mooski heard since he woke up in the dungeon. "Who that? Come here, help me down!"

"Okay, here I come," the voice came from a little girl.

He felt at ease knowing that he wasn't alone in the dungeon, then all of a sudden, he wished he was alone again. The little girl was the same one that he'd accidentally shot. As she walked closer, he could see the big bullet hole in her face. His adrenaline started pumping, and he began to panic. He tried to pull himself up again to undo the restraints, and he succeeded this time, but when he touched his ankles there was nothing there.

The next thing he knew, he was falling. He should've hit the floor already, but there wasn't one there. He just kept falling and falling.

"Ahhhh! Stop! Stop it! You lil' bitch! I'll kill you again!" he yelled psychotically.

Babie sat up on the bed with the covers clutched over her naked body looking down at Mooski frightened by what she was seeing.

He was literally suffering. She tried waking him up when he was moaning and tossing around, but she backed up when he started yelling and grabbing at the air.

"Babbbyyy! Moooskkkiii! Get up, baby!" she screamed at the top of her lungs with tears in her eyes.

He popped up like a vampire fresh out the casket. His mouth was wide open, and he was breathing heavily. He was shivering, and warm tears were rolling down his face.

He looked at Babie and at the moment, he seemed so innocent to her. She scooted up to him and put the covers over his body. "Awww, baby, you shivering."

"Get off me." He snatched away from her and got up out of the bed.

"Where you going?" she asked as he got dressed in front of her.

"I'll be back, text me if you need me."

Toe-Tag woke up this time feeling like the Devil himself. Whoever was at his door now had it coming this time.

"Whattt?" he barked as he snatched the door open.

He saw Mooski standing at his door with a mug meaner than his. "Wassup, lil' bro?" he asked in a softer voice.

Mooski walked past him without saying a word. He plopped down on the couch with his head to the ground.

"You just caught another body?" asked Toe-Tag after taking a seat on the arm of the other couch. Mooski shook his head. "You gon' have to talk to me, shawty. I don't speak no sign language."

Mooski swallowed the lump in his throat, and told him all about the dream, and how he felt when he was about to wake up, and after he had woken up. "I felt like I was about to die, man."

Toe-Tag looked at him with a smirk.

"You think this shit a joke?" he asked accusingly.

"Not at all. I'm smiling because yo' hardheaded ass thought this shit was a joke, nigga. I told you this shit was gon' take a toll on yo' soul. That right there, what you just witnessed tonight was the tip of the iceberg, it's only gon' get worse. Why you think I be trying to stay up days at a time?"

He got up, went to the back and came back with a sack of white powder. He dumped the eight-ball on the table and put a McDonald's straw in Mooski's hand. "Don't look at me like that, nigga. I'm tryin' to help yo' ass. It ain't gon' give you yo' soul back, but it'll make you feel alive while you on it."

Mooski gave in, he needed something to help cope with the madness. If that powder could lift him out of the dark place he was in, then he was all for it. He leaned down with the straw to his nose and inhaled a big bump of the powder. "Wooo-shit, damn!" His eyes was wider than Peter Griffin.

Toe-Tag snatched the straw away from him. "It ain't gon' be no fun if I don't go up with you." He bent down and put a big dent in the small mountain of pleasure. "Welcome to hell, young nigga," he joked with his head back so the drug could drain into his system.

CHAPTER 21

"Man, you might as well cut this shit off," Black said while looking down at Quay's head.

"I came over here for a lineup, nigga, not advice," Quay retorted playfully.

They were in Black's kitchen. Quay sat in a foldable chair while Black stood over him preparing to do his thing. He learned how to cut hair growing up, so G-Baby could always have a nice haircut going to school even if his shit was raggedy.

"I should start charging yo' ass for this shit," he threatened while cleaning the clippers.

"What you should do is start a barbershop called *DG cuts*, or some shit."

He stopped mid-stride and stared off into space. "That sounds good, but shit too good to be true. Toe-Tag just gave Handsome a pass. He ain't gon' give two passes in a row."

"You never know. We got enough manpower out here. Plus, Kapo got something going on with the sheriff, and he gon' basically pay us to sit down somewhere."

Black went to work on his head. "That's wassup right there. How much you think it'll cost to start a barbershop?"

"You asking the wrong person. Just hop back in the game, stack yo' paper for a while, and you'll have more than enough."

"You ain't talk to Handsome since he left?"

"Hell nah, but I saw his post on IG. Nigga looks happy as fuck."

"I bet." He pushed Quay's head down so he could temp the back. "We got to get up out this hood, bro'."

"You can go, but my black ass gon' be in the hood until it's over with."

Black shook his head disappointedly. The whole point of hustling was to do better, but niggas had the game fucked up.

The street mentality was starting to become immature to him. During recovery, he had a lot of time to reflect on shit. His perception was totally different towards a lot of things now. "Whatever floats your boat, but I'm gon' get my black ass up out this hood. I want a better life for my kids."

***

"That fuck nigga Silent been in my dreams like a mutha-fucka lately," Monster informed truthfully.

He and Dead Shot were building a strong brotherly bond. The more time they spent with each other, the more they noticed just how similar they were. They were two lieutenants trying to make it in a dirty world.

They were walking through Lennox mall with a few shooters from their kill teams tailing them.

Dead Shot looked over at him awkwardly. "Me too, shawty. I ain't even gon' flex," he admitted.

"Wait, hold on. That nigga been in your dreams, too?"

"Hell yeah, I be having other dreams too, but he always pop-up somewhere. He don't never say shit, he just be standing there lookin' evil as fuck with black eyes."

Monster stopped dead in his tracks.

"What?" Dead Shot asked.

"That's the same shit I be seeing in my dreams. You know that nigga used to fuck with them, dead people."

Dead Shot started walking again. "I ain't trying to hear that shit. You know how this shit go. I know he ain't the first person you done whacked that popped in your dreams."

"I ain't never dreamed about none of 'em this much. This on some every-night shit."

"Then why he in my dreams, then? I ain't whack the nigga."

"Because you put him in the dirt, nigga. I bet if we go ask everybody that had something to do with it, they gon' say they saw that nigga in they dreams. Something going on, shawty."

It was Dead Shot who stopped this time. "If they say that I'll give you ten gees."

"Bet!"

Dead shot shrugged. "Let's say you right. What we gon' do, call Ghost Busters?"

"We gon' have to go see a Voodoo priest or some shit. I don't know."

"You need to keep yo' nose clean 'cause that shit got you trippin', big bro'."

Monster nodded. "We gon' see."

Four hours later, they pulled up to Gilmore's warehouse on the outskirts of Athens, Georgia. This time he was waiting for them in his lobby dressed in a hot, orange, silk suit. The sun had gone down, and he was hosting a party of some sort. Beautiful Armenian women strutted around half-naked entertaining his men.

Monster was still amazed by the beautiful place even though it was his second time seeing it, but not nearly as amazed as, Dead Shot, who was witnessing its beauty for the first time.

"Gentlemen! Gentlemen! Welcome to my place. I assume you're here on behalf of Toe-Tag?" They nodded. "Come, take a seat. First, we talk business. Then we party."

He led them to a secluded section for VIPs. They all sat down, and a waitress brought them drinks immediately. "I like how you guys handled my competition out here. I've just decided to expand my business out to Miami, but I have some competition that needs to be handled out there. I was wondering if you guys would be capable of handling a job of this capacity?"

127

Dead Shot looked at Monster, and Monster looked at Gilmore. "I don't know, you'll have to give me a full detailed profile on the person. Then I'll still have to check in with Toe-Tag before we do anything."

"Understandable, but I still don't understand how someone so young obtained so much power, but I guess he's earned it. Anyway, that works, because it'll take me a few weeks to get everything straightened out, by that time you should be ready. I'll give you the file on him before you leave."

"Cool."

"Now, it's time to party!" He lifted his hands and clapped them together.

Even though the claps couldn't be heard over the disco music, six beautiful vixens strutted into the section to entertain them. "What do you think?" Gilmore asked expectantly.

Monster smiled devilishly. "Perfect, it's perfect." He grabbed the thickest woman he could find and pulled her down onto his lap.

CHAPTER 22

Toe-Tag and Mooski were still up in the living room playing *Call of Duty* on the Xbox 360. They were high out of their minds focused on the game when someone started knocking on the door.

"I wish a nigga would leave me the fuck alone!" he complained after putting the game on pause and going to the door.

He opened the door and stood face-to-face with Freddy. He was taken aback by his presence. "You got some balls pullin' up out here on my doorstep."

Freddy smiled, he found Toe-Tag amusing. Unlike everybody else, he wasn't scared of him, or any of his goons. He raised, Vonte one of the hardest niggas to ever claim Dilluminati. It was going to take more than a little trail of bodies to intimidate him. "This 'my' city. I go wherever the fuck I want."

"Please tell me what the fuck it is that you want? Ain't shit for us to talk about."

"Damn, I can't remember the last time a nigga done talked to me like that. But you know why I'm gon' let that go? Because I know, like everybody else, you don't know no better, and obviously don't care about getting whacked."

"You got four seconds to tell me what you want before I slam this door in yo' face," he threatened seriously.

"Nah, don't do that. I came all this way to tell you this personally. I could've sent a notice, but what would be the fun in that?"

"Say what you got to say and get the fuck on."

Freddy smirked smugly. "I know you love this here apartment a lot because you've been holed up in it for a little while now, but you're going to have to crawl up out of this hole, and so is everyone else in these apartments."

"What?"

"Yeah, as of twelve days ago, I'm the newfound owner of Eagle Run. As of three days ago, I've decided to have these raggedy-ass buildings torn down, so I can have some better ones built. You have six months to find you another home, for your whole camp."

The joy in Freddy's voice as he dealt that devastating blow, made Toe-Tag's blood boil. He obviously went through all that trouble to get back at him in a way that wouldn't violate DG laws. Even in his devastation and anger, he had to tilt his hat to Freddy. That was a real boss-move he'd just pulled.

"When you choose to wage war on somebody. You need to learn the enemy, as well as his allies."

Toe-Tag kept his head held high and refused to show any signs of defeat. "You got that. I was tired of the scenery anyway. I might just buy us a nice lil' apartment complex with a pool, or some shit. My Baby Gangster's would love that."

"Just make sure you do it within six months."

"You got it, old school." He slammed the door in Freddy's face.

When Monster got back to the hood, Toe-Tag was on his couch eating pork chops. "Don't you got yo' own apartment?" he asked before grabbing one of the pork chops off his plate.

"Ain't nobody gon' have no apartment in a minute. Not in Eagle Run anyway."

"What the hell you talkin' about?" He sat down next to his little brother.

Toe-Tag gave him the whole rundown on the unsettling conversation with Freddy.

"Damn," Monster said in surprise. "I wonder how much a set of apartments cost?"

"Wait, that's it!" Toe-Tag exclaimed excitedly. "You big muthafucka! You always get my mental juices flowing!" he joked seriously while struggling to put his tight-fitting Alexander McQueen jacket because he was moving too fast.

He walked toward the door and saw Monster still sitting. "Come on."

"Man, I just got in. I been ripping-and-running for two days straight, no rest."

"A'ight, hold shit down. I'm gon' take Mooski with me." He slammed the door shut behind him and rushed to his car that he finally got out of the shop.

Toe-Tag stood on Pablo's doorstep, with Mooski, ringing the doorbell repeatedly. Being annoying on purpose. A curvy Indian woman in her mid-forties answered the door. "Yes. How may I help you?"

"Go get Pablo for me."

She frowned slightly. "I'm very sorry, but he just left out not too long ago. I think he said something 'bout a blue fire or something."

He looked at Mooski amusingly, then back at the lady. "He at the Blue Flame, it's a strip club. I take it you, not his woman?" He looked her up-and-down approvingly. For an old school bitch, she did well for herself.

"Oh, no. I'm just a maid, mister."

He pulled out his phone and snapped a picture of her. She was caught off-guard by the sudden flash. Then he sent the picture to Pablo with a text saying that he'd be waiting on him.

He forced past the lady who tried to prevent him from coming in. "Stop, I'll have to call the police!"

"Then I'll be going to jail for your murder."

She loved the money and benefits she got from her job, but it wasn't worth her life. She closed the door and went on about her business.

***

Pablo came storming into his house with his security in front of him with their guns drawn. He knew all about, Toe-Tag and didn't know what the psychopath had up his greasy sleeve, so he was on edge. They found him in the dining room with one of his henchmen eating shrimp Alfredo that his maid must've prepared.

She came rushing into the room with her cooking apron on and a worried expression on her face. "I'm sorry, boss! They—"

Pablo held his hand up, making her stop talking, then waved it dismissively, signaling her to leave.

"You mind telling these toy cops to get them guns out our faces?" Toe-Tag asked with a mouth full of food.

Pablo motioned for them to put the guns down, and they obliged. "Why you can't never just call, and set up a meeting like regular people? You always got to do some extreme ass shit."

"Do I look like a regular nigga to you?"

Pablo didn't answer. He just told his men to give them some privacy and took a seat at the table. "Get to the part where you tell me what you want."

Toe-Tag shrugged nonchalantly and dropped his fork on the plate with a clinging noise. "Fuck it. Yo' bitch can't cook like that anyway. Remember that favor we had in between us?"

"Favor? Nah, I don't recall no shit like that," he lied sarcastically.

"Play with this, Pablo."

"Yeah, man. What you want?" He couldn't wait to get the menace out of his hair.

"Find out who owns Sun Valley Apartments and make him sell it to you."

Pablo frowned. "Why the hell would I do that?"

"Because I'm telling you to, but you can't ever sell it. After that, we gon' be even." He went on and told Pablo about his predicament because he knew he would ask.

"Damn, that nigga there don't play, but I got you. Y'all niggas better be on time for rent *every* month, or I'm gone evict all y'all asses!" he joked, but nobody laughed with him.

"I'm gon' pay *everybody's* rent, at once, in cash every month," he assured confidently.

"I see why them folks love you so much. They get to live for free," he joked again.

Toe-Tag stood up, followed by Mooski. "Handle that business and let me know when it's done."

"Them apartments just got redone. What if they don't go for it?"

It was only then that Toe-Tag smiled. "Let me know if I need to give 'em some convincing. They gon' sell that shit one way or another."

Malik D. Rice

CHAPTER 23

"I'm surprised they put you on my visitation list. Who you paid to get that done?" Mazi asked Toe-Tag. He was the bigger, and badder version of Toe-Tag.

They sat in the visitation room at Smith State Prison attracting a lot of attention. Toe-Tag took it upon himself to pull up in three rented Lamborghinis. He drove in the red one, and the four Mobsters that he brought with him drove the white, and blue ones. Mazi was sure to be the talk of the prison after this.

"Man, you worried about the wrong shit. Just be happy somebody coming to see yo' ugly ass," Toe-Tag joked.

"Got me fucked up, lil' nigga. I got three badass hoes on my list."

Toe-Tag made a face. "Your bad and my bad is two totally different things."

"Fuck you. Wassup, though? How you been holdin' up? Yo' name ringing bells in them streets. I'm proud of you because you handling business and taking care of your own, but I ain't trying to lose you to them streets. They say you the new, Vonte, out there."

"Who is *they*? They damn sure talk a lot."

"I'm serious lil' bro. You need to slow yo ass down."

Toe-Tag picked up a bag of Cool Ranch Doritos off the small coffee table that separated them. "You ain't gon' eat?"

"I just ate three burgers and a pizza. I'm full, nigga. Now, answer my question. What you got going on out there?"

Since he was asking for it, Toe-Tag sat right there, and laid-out everything he was currently going through. When he was finished a whole hour had passed just that fast.

"Damn, young nigga. My lil' brother a real Crime Lord. I'm proud of you, bro'."

Toe-Tag waved him off. "Fuck all that, I seen them tattoos you been posting on Instagram. You got some good work. I'm gon' have to buy you a tattoo shop when you get home because you ain't goin' back to them streets."

"I know you a made-man and all that good shit, but you still my lil' brother. I'm gon' be right there next to you, and Monster, making sure y'all straight."

Toe-Tag shook his head. "You heard from that lawyer I got you lately?"

"Yeah, that lady the truth. It's looking real good. If she gets this life sentence dropped to ten years, I'm gon' marry her ugly ass," he joked.

"You hell. You coming home, though. I don't care if I got to drop a million on yo' case."

Mazi looked at his little brother proudly. "DG." It meant *I love you.*

"L4E." *I love you, too!*

***

AK stood on the back of a U-Haul truck with a few Mobsters unloading mini dirt bikes, four-wheelers, and motorcycles. All the Baby Mobsters in the hood crowded the truck excited like it was Christmas all over again.

One of AK's songs was blasting from the truck. It was a club banger that he'd just dropped. Dinero Girls and kids were dancing in the middle of the street enjoying themselves.

"I'ma put the Mob on, bitch
Make sure that we all get rich
Niggas still killing in the field
That's just the way it issss—"

Toe-Tag walked outside in a tight, black-and-white Adidas jumpsuit. "What the hell goin' on out here?" he asked one of the Young Mobsters who was posted up with a few more.

"AK, doing the right thing, and I respect it."

"Come on," he said while walking towards the U-Haul with the Mobsters in tow.

AK smiled when he saw Toe-Tag walking up. He hopped off the truck and walked up to him. "What's good, Don?" They dapped each other up.

"Chaos as usual. What you got going on out here?" he asked after telling the Mobsters to go help unload the truck.

"Just giving back to the hood, that's all. Lighten the load for you a lil' bit. I was hearing about all the shit you was doin' for them, and I started feeling bad. From now on, I'm going to do my part, on top of the dues I'm paying you. That's on the 4s."

"Started feeling bad? The AK I remember ain't have no conscience," he joked.

"I know right, but when Rampage took my spot, that shit tore me down, and I rebuilt myself humbly. I noticed how fucked up of a person I was because folks wasn't scared to tell me then. You, and Rampage, done showed me a lot bro'."

"Word, I'm glad you made a change for the better, shawty. I'm proud of you, we all is. Keep going, my nigga."

"I ain't gon' never stop."

"Do me a favor."

"Anything for you, Don."

"Write another letter to Rampage on one of them songs. I listen to the first one every day."

Ak smiled brightly. "Say no more, I'm working on this mixtape with, 21 Savage, so I'll just put it on there."

Malik D. Rice

CHAPTER 24

There was an advanced training facility in the mountains of Ohio. It was run by a man that went by the name, Dreads. He was one of the best mercenaries to ever step foot on American soil, but he wasn't American. He was Haitian. He wasn't kin, but he was a close friend of Mr. Follian.

You could only get admitted into the facility by referral, and even then, you had to pay the admission fee, which as $75,000 bi-annually. Vonte went ahead and paid for a whole year for himself, Facts, and Millie. The lessons were pricey, but they would come in handy for what Vonte had planned for the future.

The entire facility was underground, and literally built inside one of the mountains. There was a big, steel, false wall on the mountain that could be opened electronically, or manually. It slid up like a garage door. Once the door was open, there was a long hallway that led to an elevator that took you down to the facility. It was humongous with two levels. The living quarters were on the first level, and the training quarters were on the lower second level.

Training hours were from 4:00 a.m. all the way to 4:00 p.m., from Monday through Saturday. Fortunately, they got to take Sundays off. The first month was the hardest for most students.

"Man, fuck this shit! I'm too old for this shit. No pussy, or drugs for a year? We might as well be locked up!" Facts complained seriously.

There were currently twenty students training at the facility at the time, and all of them had their own small rooms, and a bathroom with a shower inside. Facts, and Millie, was chilling in Vonte's room after a *long* day of training.

"It's called self-discipline. When we leave out this bitch. We gone be like John Wick on these niggas. If we gon' do something, might as well be the best at what we do," said Vonte while texting one of his hoes.

"Fuck all that. No drugs, and pussy! It's four females training with us, and three on the staff team. You telling me I can't get jiggy with none of 'em?"

"Hell no! And yo' ugly ass better not try either. Them the rules, and we gon' abide by 'em. Y'all here on my face, so if y'all fuck up, I fuck up. I ain't gon' fuck up cause y'all' ain't gon' fuck up," the seriousness in his voice couldn't be missed. This was very important to him.

"Whatever, I'm about to go watch me a porno, and jack my dick," Facts informed before leaving out of the room.

Vonte looked at Millie who sat in the corner with his back to the wall, on his phone as well. "What you doin' over there, pretty boy?"

"Same thing you doing, nigga."

"Alexis?"

He couldn't stop the smile. "Yeah, mainly. Who you talking to, Violence?"

"Mannn—"

"What?"

Vonte looked at him through sad eyes. "Shawty just disappeared off the face of the earth. Can't *nobody* tell me where she at. I think Toe-Tag got a hold of her."

***

There was a basketball game at McNair high school, and it was jam-packed. The McNair Mustangs were playing the Lithonia Bulldogs. Toe-Tag and a bunch of Mobsters were in the building putting on for the hood. The starting point guard for the Mustangs was from their hood. He was a sixteen-year-old boy named, Dontavious. He had mob-ties because of where he grew up, but he wasn't affiliated. He was a good kid with a true gift on the court.

A local rapper from Lithonia had made an announcement after performing at the halftime show, saying he had $2,500 on the Bulldogs, so Toe-Tag being the nigga he was, told the nigga to bet $5,000 after slapping a wad of money on the ground nonchalantly. The rapper was hesitant, but couldn't back down in front of the crowd, so he agreed.

Toe-Tag and the rest of the Mobsters that had shown up with him were standing on the side of the bleachers since all the seats in the house were full.

The Mustangs were down six points in the fourth quarter with two minutes left in the game. Dontavious had a lot of pressure on him because his first-string center was hurt, so they were short on rebounds. Plus, the Bulldogs had an elite team on top of that.

His favorite NBA player was Chris Paul because they favored one another. The only difference is that he didn't have hazel eyes and wore his hair in a nappy temped fro. He came up the court breathing hard because he was tired as hell. He basically played the whole game, only taking a short three-minute break.

The point guard from the other team was waiting for him at the half-court-line. He was on Dontavious' ass because he knew how lethal his jump shot was, so he put his best defense in play in hopes that he would pass the ball.

Dontavious hit him with a few crossovers, and then came the shooting guard from the other team. He was being double-teamed. He looked up at the clock and saw nine seconds left on the shot-clock. He bounced the ball, took a step forward to draw the foul, then hopped back while putting the ball in the air.

"Dlattt!" The Mobsters barked in unison as the ball sunk inside the net perfectly.

The crowd went crazy as three points were added onto the board, and Dontavious went to the free-throw line. Dontavious looked up at the clock, looked over at his mother in the stands with his little sister, and blew them a kiss, before throwing the ball up and making the shot without taking his eyes off his family.

The crowd cheered again.

"I'm gon' make sure this nigga go to the best college they got! He gon' go to the NBA, and put on for the hood, shawty," Toe-Tag told Mooski who stood right beside him.

He'd been spending a lot of time with Toe-Tag lately since Monster hooked up with Dead Shot. "Facts, I might chip in. That young nigga definitely going places."

"A'ight, hold on. They back in motion"

Dontavious put the full-court press on the other point-guard as he made his way up the court. They only needed two points to win, so he passed the ball to their power forward who had gone in for a lay-up and missed.

The Mustangs got the ball, and of course, it ended up in Dontavious' hands. He took the fast break, and his power forward just so happened to be in front of him. He thought about passing it but didn't feel like going through the hassle of overtime. He had a TV show to catch tonight, so he went for the gusto.

He took three long steps past the half-court line, stopped, jumped, and shot the ball nonchalantly. He landed on the ground before the ball landed, and turned around walking toward the other goal, not even watching to see if he was going to make it. When the crowd started going bananas, he smiled and threw up Dilluminati with his tongue sticking out.

Toe-Tag collected his money happily.

Forty-five minutes later, Dontavious was walking in the parking lot with his mother and little sister.

Toe-Tag and all the Mobsters that were at the game with him lounged around their Escalades that were parked right next to his mother's Acura. "Good game, lil' nigga," Toe-Tag said before giving him the extra $5,000 he won off the game. "That's for you."

"Damn, thank you, big bro'," said Dontavious right behind his mother, who beat him to the punch. She didn't agree with what he did but wasn't about to turn down free money.

"That ain't shit. Keep getting good grades and playing ball how he been playing. I'm gon' keep paying you. That's yo' job. Alright?"

Dontavious smiled brightly. "Alright, I won't let you down."

"You won't let 'us' down. It ain't just me, everybody counting on you."

Malik D. Rice

CHAPTER 25

~Five months later~

Pablo held up his end of the deal and bought Sun Valley Apartments. It took a few visits and indirect threats, but the owner wisely gave in after a few months, but it got done, and Toe-Tag moved everybody from his old hood to Sun Valley. The only person that didn't move with them is, Jasmine. She signed her deal with DG Books and had a little steady income, so she moved out to a nice little apartment in Lithonia. She was tired of the hood.

In a way, Freddy did them a favor because Sun Valley was bigger, better, and right next to Paradise East Apartments. Now it made the bond they had with PDE that much stronger because the two apartments were literally right next to each other. They were one big family now.

Toe-Tag gave all his old furniture away and had expensive items imported from overseas. He had the walls to the apartment next to his knocked down and turned it into one big super-apartment. When the renovations were done, it looked like an upscale condo. It was his home he had no plans on moving out of the hood anytime soon, if ever.

The best part about the ordeal is that he let his mother, and sister, stay in the house he had them hidden out at, and Shanay chose to move into the new spot with him. She wanted Lil' Tee to be around his father, that he loved more than her if you let her tell it.

He sat on the stool with his back to the kitchen watching her play with him and the Teacup Poodle he'd bought for them. It was an expensive dog that could fit in the palm of your hand at its full size. He remembered hearing her tell his mother that she wanted one and surprised her with it when she showed up with Lil' Tee.

He made them leave all their belongings and bought them brand new everything because it was a brand-new start for them. They had on matching Gucci, Polo shirts he'd bought for all three of them. They were waiting on the photographer, so he could take family pictures of them. It's been three days since they showed up, and shit had been excellent.

Shanay caught him watching them, and left Lil' Tee on the floor playing with the dog. She walked up to, Toe-Tag right in between his legs. "Hey."

"Wassup, lil' mamma? You like the new spot?"

"Yes, I love it. You know that because I've told you a million times. I took a picture yesterday, and my sister swears that I moved downtown in a condo or some shit."

"That's what it is, a condo in the hood. That's why I got it on the top floor, to make it feel like a condo in the sky even though we ain't that high," he joked.

She touched his sexy baby face softly and let her hands glide on his smooth skin. "It's perfect, baby. I'm just glad you're ready to start spending more time with me, and Lil' Tee."

"Yeah, I don't be in the field no more. I let Monster call the shots now. All I do is sit back, and plot now."

"That's what bosses do, baby. DG," she said before leaning in for a quick kiss.

"L4E, now and foreva."

***

Mooski and Babie was on a double date with Kamya and Handsome. Everybody knows how much Kamya loves movies, so they went to the movie theaters, now they were at *Gladice Chicken and Waffles* in the same plaza as Stonecrest Mall.

"So, how the square life treating you, my nigga?" Mooski asked Handsome. He saw a change in him. He seemed happier now.

"Shit wonderful, more money, and less problems," he answered truthfully.

Babie looked at Mooski. "I can make Toe-Tag give you a pass too, baby. You want to do that?"

"Come on, man, I'm a shooter. I love the action. I wouldn't jump camps if Toe-Tag tried to make me. He just gon' have to kill me."

Babie shook her head. "Talk some sense into this stupid ass nigga here."

"It ain't gon' do no good. Before I started fuckin' with Kamya, it wasn't nothing a nigga could tell me. He gon' be good, though. Toe-Tag gon' take real good care of him."

Mooski waved them off. "Fuck all that. How much you done made already?"

"A couple hundred thousand. I really just got done paying dues. Plus, I'm making investments and shit. So, the money about to start piling up a lot more now."

"That's wassup. I got investments too, nigga," he said jokingly.

"Oh, yeah, in what?"

"I just bought a rocket launcher. That bitch kick harder than Goku!" Mooski answered smiling grimly.

After the dinner date, they went their separate ways. Babie, and Mooski, pulled up in his black-on-black 2012 Camero that he had sitting up on shiny black 26-inch rims. They were on the highway on the way back to the hood when Babie brought the subject up again. "You sure you don't want to jump camps?

It'll be good not to have to worry about you when you go out on missions, and shit."

He glanced over at her, then focused back on the road causing his dreads to do a little dance. "Man, you need to kill that shit. I ain't nothing like that other nigga you was fuckin' with, who couldn't stand up in the paint. I'm really built for this shit. I'm gon' be straight. And if I die, fuck it. I'll be wit' my mamma, and daddy, in hell."

His parents used to pull capers together around the city of Atlanta until they took off the wrong people, and it eventually ended up catching up with them.

She just sat there looking out the window thinking about her brother. She knew he would've approved of Mooski because he used to talk highly of him, but she really didn't want to lose him. She was one of those females that needed a gangster man in her life, and Mooski was the definition. He was quickly becoming Toe-Tag's top shooter with six bodies on his belt already.

"Baby."

"Yeah."

"If you die, I'm gon' turn gay."

He laughed without replying.

CHAPTER 26

Monster woke up to ZyAsia's face. She was just sitting there with her legs crossed on the bed staring at him.

"What the hell wrong with you man? What I tell you about that shit?"

"Whattt, I can't look at my nigga?"

He sat up in the bed, picked up a half-smoked blunt of weed off the nightstand, and fired it up. "Yeah, but—not like that. That shit creepy as fuck. You already got them big ass eyes."

"Shut up!" she spat while hitting him playfully. "Look."

He squinted his eyes at the white stick. It was a pregnancy test. "What, your sister pregnant?"

"No! I'm pregnant, stupid!"

He looked at her sideways. "I thought you was on birth control?"

"Well—I was, but you kept saying you ain't want no kids, and—"

"And what, Asia?" his voice boomed so hard it made her jump. "You pulled a lil' sneaky ass move like that?"

"I just wanted a babbyyy! What if you die out there in them streets? I ain't gon' have no part of you to hold on to. Plus, we ain't getting no younger."

Monster took a deep breath and knocked the lamp off the nightstand as he exhaled causing it to break on the hardwood floor. "How the fuck I'm supposed to trust you when you out here pulling sneaky ass moves like that?" He got up and started putting on his clothes.

"Where you going?" She got up and tried to pull him back down onto the bed.

He pushed her down back onto the bed. "Leave me alone, Asia."

She got off the bed and started getting dressed with him. "I'm going, too."

"You ain't going nowhere. You know I'm overprotective, and you got my baby in yo' stomach. You gon' keep it safe, in this apartment."

"So, you telling me I can't leave this apartment for seven months?"

He stopped in the middle of tying his shoe. "Damn, you two months already." She nodded. "Shit crazy." He grabbed everything he needed and left.

"Wassup, Monster? Why you looking mad, big bro'? Need me to whack a nigga for you?" one of the Baby Mobsters asked as he made his way down the stairs of his building. His name was, Quavo. He spent all twelve years of his life in the hood and Monster knew his whole family.

"You need to take yo' lil' ass to school," said Monster after dapping him up.

It was a nice, sunny day and Quavo didn't have on anything but a pair of cut-off black Robin Jeans, and a pair of black Prada shoes with straps. He stood at 5'9, weighing 120 pounds. "It's summertime, ain't no school."

"Well, take yo' ass somewhere, and do something. Yo' mamma gon' kill me if I put you in the game."

"You know, just like she knows, that I'm gon' hop in the game anyway. I'm twelve, and all my friends got bumped up to Young Mobsters. Why I got to be the only twelve-year-old Baby Mobster in the hood?"

Monster looked at the little nigga long and hard. He was growing up, and he did have a right to be in the game. This was his hood. "Come take a ride with me, lil' nigga."

They hopped inside Monster's new 2015 black-on-black Range Rover.

New to the Game 2

Two hours later, they were in front of a house in Stone Mountain. It was a drug house that peddled weed, and cocaine. They weren't big time, but they made ends meet.

"What's the move?" Quavo asked from the passenger seat.

"Listen, don't shit in this world come free, but oxygen. Everything else got its price. The price of jumping into the game got is taking risks." He put a loaded 9mm. in his lap. "That's loaded with one in the head, and the safety's off so all you got to do is pull the trigger, but only if you got to. This ain't no hit, it's a robbery. You see them niggas on that corner right there?" He nodded. "Go run all they pockets. Remember, don't shoot unless you see a nigga pulling out a gun."

Quavo didn't even hesitate before grabbing the gun, opening the door, and sneaking up the street just like he practiced.

Monster sat back and prepared himself for the show. He had his AR-15 in his lap just in case he had to come to the rescue. He was aware that Quavo could get hurt, but if he jumped in the game, he would be taking a lot more chances with his life. It was part of the game. Plus, he knew the niggas weren't about that life for real, which is why he drove out there.

Quavo closed in on the group of dealers. There were four of them, and two of them were wearing the new Jordans that he wanted, and one of them looked like they wore his size. "Y'all *fuck-niggas* strip!" his voice boomed harder than it ever did. He surprised himself.

The fact that he was barefaced with an extended clip in his gun had them worried. Despite the fact that this was his first caper, he looked comfortable doing it like it was his daily job. He had malice in his eyes, and his hand wasn't shaking a bit. It was solid as a rock.

"Make me say it one more time!"

Luckily for them, they didn't try to call his bluff because he was definitely going to whack one of them right there where they stood. "Naked! I want everything, but the draws." One of them sucked their teeth. "Matter-of-fact, come on with the boxers, too! Y'all can thank this stupid ass nigga," he said while pointing the gun at the youngest one out there.

They were undressing slowly.

"Hurry the fuck up, put everything in a pile!"

They did as they were told, and ten seconds later everything was in a pile.

"Now run down the street as fast as y'all can. If you turn around, I got seventeen bullets in this bitch, and they gon' fly."

They took off running down the street like track stars.

"Sweeettt!" Quavo stuck the gun in his pocket and scooped their pants, guns, and one pair of Jordans up before jogging back to the car.

"What the fuck you lookin' at, old school?" He barked at an old lady who had her head sticking out her door. She hurried and went back inside.

"Dlattt!" he shouted as he got back in the truck with Monster.

Monster was laughing hard. "You did that, lil' nigga. You did that."

CHAPTER 27

There was a $27 million mega yacht crushing smoothly on the blue waters of the Pacific Ocean. Two dozen unbelievably beautiful models of all sizes, and races, lounged throughout the boat doing their jobs, looking pretty. There was no guarantee, but if, 2-Tall decided to choose one of them for entertainment, then they were lucky.

He stood on the upper level on a balcony attached to his condo overlooking the beautiful women swim naked in the water, do drugs, and converse with one another. His security, which consisted of a small army, was all throughout the boat at different checkpoints constantly communicating with each other through state-of-the-art earpieces.

He wore Burberry swim trunks with white Versace slides, and a pair of gold-rimmed Cartier reading glasses on. He only had on a few small chains, but they were nearly a million dollars apiece. He was currently the biggest Drug Lord on the East Coast.

"It took me a minute to get used to this life, you know. I met, Malina, and my life has never been the same since. Don't get it twisted, I had a few hundred thousand before we met, but that ain't shit in my eyes now. Look at this shit! I just bought a thirty-million-dollar yacht with no pressure."

Kapo stood next to him dressed more professionally in white Armani pants, a thin light grey Louis Vuitton dress shirt with the sleeves rolled up, and a pair of dark, grey, patent leather Mauri gators on his size ten feet. "Yeah, you doing good. I'm still trying to get used to the few millions I'm making, so I know you still adjusting to hundreds of millions with the time span of a year. That's insane."

2-Tall smiled. "It's crazy because my bitch just hit a billion herself, and she talking about marriage."

"What you gon' do?"

"I'm gon' marry the bitch! I'll be a damn fool if I didn't. Plus, I'm scared the Cartel gon' whack me if I don't."

Kapo waved him off. "They ain't gon' kill you. You making them too much money. Think of them as the Illuminati, and us, as the Masons. They can't enjoy the luxury of sitting back on their asses without us handling the groundwork for them."

"You a deep muthafucka, Kapo. That's why I fuck with you."

Malina's Ferragamo heels were clinking on the marble floor as she made her way toward them. She was dressed beautifully in a white, see-through, summer dress, and a Burberry bikini up under. "Heyyy, my beautiful fiance."

They both turned around facing her and leaned their backs on the rail. "What I tell you about that beautiful shit? A man is handsome, or sexy. Shit, I'll take cute, or adorable, but beautiful ain't gon' cut it, baby."

"Okay, okayyy, I won't embarrass you in front of your friend here," she said while glancing in Kapo's direction.

"This is my nigga, Kapo. The new Godfather of Georgia."

***

"Shit, I don't give a fuck. I'm just glad they ain't whack me. I'm straight with being the Pope anyway," said Masio truthfully. "That Godfather shit too political for me, and I damn sure ain't no politician."

They were having their traditional dinner at Bizzy's.

"What do you do besides collect money? How the hell did you get this far up anyway?" Freddy asked although he knew the answer. Drop Top and Masio were like strippers and poles. They went together greatly.

"Anyway. You heard from your nephew?"

"Which one? The superstar, or the Devil?"

"The Devil."

"Yeah, only on Instagram, though. Never seen him face-to-face after that night."

"That's the only nigga in DG history to buck a death-sentence. He and Ronte got to be some kind of special."

"It's in they bloodline, nigga. You ain't know?"

Masio dipped his hand inside of the cup of water that sat in front of him and flicked the water at Freddy. "Shut up, nigga. My lil' brother about to drop that New To The Game. Make sure you buy forty-four copies."

"Who, Santana? He done signed that publishing deal for real?"

"Yup," Masio answered while smiling proudly.

"I'm proud of that nigga there. What the lawyer talking about on his case?"

"It's looking good. He got another court date coming up soon. The state fucked up on his case bad, so my lil' nigga definitely coming home."

Freddy nodded his head approvingly. "So, wassup? What you trying to do after this? Let's go to the strip club."

"How you gon' ask me where I want to go, then suggest some shit?"

"Alright. Where you want to go, big baby?"

He acted like he was in deep thought with a hand cupping his chin looking off into space. Thirty seconds later, he had an answer, "Let's hit the strip club."

"Boy, I don't even know why I put up with you?"

They left the waitresses a thousand-dollar tip and made their way.

Malik D. Rice

New to the Game 2

CHAPTER 28

The Dons in Pablo's camp were having their traditional meeting. This time, they were in the backyard of Papa's new suburban house under the gazebo watching their ladies lounge in the water, getting their tans on, laying on top of their floats sipping on ice-cold mixed drinks. Everything had been running smooth lately, and they basically had all their affairs in order, so instead of a meeting, it was more of a celebration of their success.

"Toe-Tag, I'm proud of you lil' bro," Papa informed seriously.

Toe-Tag looked at him awkwardly. "For what?"

"For sitting your ass down!" he joked drawing laughter from the rest of the Dons. "Nah, real shit though. I'm proud of *everybody*. We coming a long way in this shit. Our numbers getting bigger, our money getting longer, and Spike Lee just made a movie about this mob shit! Who the fuck gon' stop us?"

"Nobody!" The rest of them said in unison.

"All we got to do is remain Loyal 4 Eva, and we gon' be straight."

***

Monster and Dead Shot had made a strong bond, and tons of money with the Armenian sensation, Gilmore. He usually didn't get too close to the African American race, but he saw something in the two mercenaries that he liked, so he associated with them outside of business.

They were at his warehouse gambling on a game of pool, $1,000 on every shot they called. "Where's your brother?" he asked Monster.

"He's handling something for me out of state."

Gilmore glanced at him knowingly.

"Nah, not that."

His face turned into a mask of disappointment.

"Come on with that shit, G." That's was the nickname he made for him. "All the shit we done did for you. It ain't like we trying to neglect you, or nothin' like that. It's just that we ain't gon' do nothing we think we can't handle, and this job you asking for is way out of our league. We barely did the last job."

A few weeks ago, Gilmore presented a $2 million job to them. He wanted them to take out a team of gun traffickers out in Vegas so he could conquer that territory. Toe-Tag paid their advanced private investigator to collect information on the individuals, and it sent up a red flag. They'd done more than enough jobs to make them professionals but on a mediocre scale. The job that Gilmore wanted them to do was for advanced professionals, and they were far from it.

"I wish you guys could pull this off for me because if I get anybody else to do this, I'll have to kill them after. Unfortunately, you guys are the only ones I trust outside of my operation."

Monster called the solid 6-ball into the corner pocket and made it. "I tell you what. You get somebody else to do the job, and we'll whack 'em for you with a discount."

"Deal. You know how much money there is to be made in Vegas?"

"No, but I know you gon' tell me."

Gilmore smiled. "Yes, my friend. Yes, I am."

"Let me find out you're becoming too attached to them," those words came out of Freddy's mouth, and he believed his accusation towards his visitor.

They were in the back of Freddy's smoky, grey BMW stretch limo. For as much money it cost him, he was basically living in it these days. He'd be damned if he didn't get his money's worth.

"You know that's not the case. You know where my loyalty lies."

"It's not me you need to be worried about, it's my nephew. When he decides to resurface. Who do you think going to be one of the first people he'll come for?"

"Just tell me what I need to do to make shit right."

"I'm going to let you know, but until then, just continue gaining their loyalty."

"Alright. You know how to get in contact with me if you need me."

"Yes, I do. I'll definitely be in touch. Now if you'll excuse me, I have places to be."

Dead Shot nodded his head and got out of the limo.

***

Black walked up to Toe-Tag's door with Quay standing right behind him. Quay had come up with the idea and persuaded him to do it, so Black made him come along.

"You gon' ring the doorbell, or you just gon' stand here looking stupid all day?" Quay asked.

Black rung the doorbell, and Shanay came to the door twenty seconds later. "Hey, y'all."

"Wassup, Shanay. Toe-Tag here?"

"Yup, he eating in the dining room. Come in." She stepped aside so they could walk in.

"Don, what the hell you got going on? We don't see too much of you no more," Black greeted.

Toe-Tag looked up at them with a smile. He missed his niggas. "I been so damn busy writing this movie script and dealing with these lawyers, and investors. Shit been crazy."

They looked at him crazily.

"Movie script? Investors? Let me find out you squaring up," Quay asked then stated.

"Just trying to do better, bro'. AK influenced me to do the movie script, and Shanay influenced me to start making legal investments, and all that good shit."

They looked at each other.

"I'm proud of you, bro'. I'm glad we on this subject because that's what I came here for," Black informed sheepishly. He was still unsure of how Toe-Tag would act.

"Oh, yeah? Talk to me. Make it quick, though. I got a video meeting in a lil' bit."

"Well—I been thinking about this for a while now. I guess this is the perfect time since shit been going smooth in the hood, and we got our numbers up."

Toe-Tag rolled his hands signaling him to cut to the chase.

"You know how I like to cut hair and shit. I was wondering if I gave you forty gees could I get a pass to become inactive, so I can buy, and run my own barbershop?"

Toe-Tag took a few bites of his spaghetti with Italian sausage inside. He took his time consuming the food as he thought about Black's request. "You'll have to pay taxes to me once the place gets up-and-running."

"That's already expected."

"A'ight. You done been through enough and put in enough work for this shit. I'll give you a pass."

Quay cheered with a fist-pump. "I told you, nigga!" He gave Black a bear hug.

"What the hell you talkin' about?" Toe-Tag asked, amused at Quay's excitement.

"This nigga thought you was gon' turn him down, but I kept telling him you was gon' fuck with him. He done put in too much work."

Toe-Tag nodded. "Y'all niggas ain't 'bout to make this no habit, though. I need somebody in the field," he joked seriously.

CHAPTER 29

Shanay ran her hand up-and-down Toe-Tag's leg. "I'm so proud of you, baby. You done turned back into the Tevin that I know. Look at you, you dressing different, and all." He still wore all black but dressed more sophisticated. He had on a Givenchy button-down shirt, Giovanni dress pants, and Mauri gators. He'd turned in to a real mob-boss.

"Who would've thought we'd make it this far? Just less than a year ago, we was trying to figure out how we was gon' get our first car, now we own a Ferarri and two AMG Benzes."

They were riding on the new Ferris-wheel downtown right by Georgia Technical College. As soon as Toe-Tag heard about it, he had to take Shanay. She liked when he did little shit with her.

"Look at our city, the shit so pretty," she admitted while looking out at the cars, buildings, and people.

"You said it right. It's 'our' city, shawty. We run this shit."

"Boy, stop your shit. Aye, baby?"

He looked over at her. "Wassup?"

"I want to have another baby. We got enough space in our condo and more than enough money. What you think?"

"I mean if that's what you want."

"It's not just about me. A relationship consists of two people. Your opinion matters too, baby."

He put a diamond-covered hand on her stomach. "We can put one in there tonight. Go pop me a molly and go crazy in that pussy."

"Now, that sounds like my kind of party," she purred seductively.

All of a sudden, they were ready to get off the ride and go home. They had business to handle.

They were on their way home in one of their AMG Benz's with an Escalade full of Mobsters behind them. Valencia was at the wheel, as usual, pretending like she wasn't listening in on their conversations.

They were discussing their plans for Lil' Tee's second birthday when Toe-Tag's mother called his phone. "Wassup, ma?"

"Boy, get your ass out here, now! A big ass tree just fell on the muthafuckin' house!" she informed angrily.

"What? Y'all alright?" he asked worriedly.

"Yeah, but you need to get your ass out here, boy!"

About an hour later, they were pulling up into his mother's driveway. "The tree must be in the back because I don't see shit," Shanay stated suspiciously.

They got out of the truck and went around the back. It was broad daylight, and they didn't even see a branch. "What kind of games this lady playing?" Toe-Tag asked angrily as he walked up the to slide door and opened it.

"Maaaa!"

Phat came downstairs with a smile on her dimpled face. "Hey, baby." She tried to pull him in for a kiss.

"Get the fuck up off me, man! Why the hell you playing like that? I was worried about y'all."

"I just wanted you to come out here. I got something to show you."

He sighed deeply while massaging his temples. "What, ma? What you tryin' to show me?"

"Go upstairs in the guest room, and you gon' see."

He rushed upstairs because his curiosity was eating away at him. It wasn't like Phat to play games like that, and she was acting extremely weird. He stopped in his sister's room and checked on her on his way to the guest room. He opened the door and found her knocked out on the bed sleep.

He smiled and closed the door back lightly before making his way down the hallway. As he neared the guest room, he heard a woman moaning loudly. Who the fuck could be in there if his mother was downstairs? He opened the guest room door and couldn't believe his eyes. He'd quit fucking around with the cocaine, so he knew he wasn't tripping. It was like looking inside of a flex-mirror that adjusted your size.

"Mazi?"

Malik D. Rice

CHAPTER 30

Mazi was on top of his girlfriend, Gina pounding away at her soaking wet pussy when his brother opened the door and interrupted. He wasn't mad though because Toe-Tag was just the person he wanted to see.

"You want some of this shit, lil' nigga? What's mine is yours." he stated without losing his stride.

Toe-Tag wasn't worried about the bitch up under him. He was curious to the fact that Mazi was literally outside of prison gates at the moment. "What you doing out? What the fuck?"

"Listen, if you ain't tryin' to hit this shit, I'm gon' need you to get yo' ass out so I can get off. I been locked up for ten years, it's been a long time," he informed while pushing Gina's long legs back even further over her head.

Toe-Tag went back downstairs and found Shanay helping his mother prepare a meal in the kitchen for them. "We cooking an early dinner for y'all," Phat informed cheerfully.

"Ma, what the fuck goin' on?"

"He gave the time back, baby. Use your head."

"I see that, but why the hell y'all ain't tell me? I would've had everything laid out for him. Now I got to rush and get everything ready for him, so he can be comfortable," he stated stressfully.

"He wanted to surprise you. The last time you went to visit him a few months ago, he knew then. He just wanted to surprise you, Tevin."

Twenty minutes later, Mazi came downstairs in a pair of basketball shorts with his shirt off displaying his muscular tattooed torso.

Shanay was grateful that Toe-Tag didn't see the look she gave Mazi upon entry. She quickly shook the deceitful thoughts out of her head and continued chopping up the peppers.

"What's all this?" he asked Toe-Tag who had a large stack of money on the counter and was now taking off all his jewelry.

"It's yours, nigga. That's thirty-five gees right there. You gots to know all them chains is water, and this right here." He took the watch off his arm. "This my new piece, but I can always get another one. It's yours, too."

Mazi stood there looking unsure. "You ain't got to give me all this shit, bro."

"Nigga, that's light work. I'm up a million-plus, so that mean you up a million. Better act like you know."

"We going out tonight?"

Toe-Tag hadn't gone out in more than six months. For a nigga like him, he felt like it wasn't really the smartest thing to do. If he wanted to party, the farthest he would go is to KINKY, but he couldn't take Mazi there for a major celebration like this. He had to do it big for his big brother. "Make it tomorrow, I got to set everything up."

"Bet!"

***

Meanwhile, in Sun Valley, Quay had just pulled up to the hood. He was coming from the mall with his kill-team. He had done a little shopping for his kids. He got back inside his apartment, sat the clothes in the living room on the floor, and went to the back to see if Diamond had come back home.

They had got into a fight because she found out that he was fucking one of the girls that she worked with, who claimed to be friends with her. She and the girl fell out, and she was gone by the time Quay had got home to make-up with her.

They'd been through this before. They'd get into it, she'd pack her stuff, leave, then eventually come back, so he wasn't too worried when he saw that she, nor her belongings, wasn't there. It's been two days now, so he'd give her a few more days before she came back home to daddy.

Two of the Young Mobsters on his kill-team had pulled a nice little caper and paid their dues to him. As of right now, he had just over $16,000 on his person, and that was too much. He wasn't like the rest of the Mafiosos, who didn't mind walking around with that much money on them, or more. He kept his bankroll under $10,000, so he didn't have to worry about the police trying to take his shit.

He went into his closet and broke down his mountain of shoeboxes, so he could get to the most important one. He kept an immediate stash in a tan Timberland shoebox. When he picked the box up and found it empty, his stomach literally dropped. "Ohhh-naaahhh, I know this hoe ain't do that? She ain't stupid like that."

All of a sudden, he dropped the shoebox in the closet and ran out of the bedroom into the kitchen. In one of the lower cabinets, he had a false bottom where he kept his *real* stash at. He snatched everything out of the cabinet hurriedly and opened the panel on the bottom.

There was a single sticky note pasted at the bottom. Nothing else. He picked the little note up and read the small neat handwriting in blue ink. It definitely came from, Diamond.

As you can see, I'm not coming back this time!

He fell back onto his ass, then eventually laid down with his back, and head on the kitchen floor looking up at the ceiling. He felt sick. That was literally *all* he had. She hit him for over a quarter-million. She knew what he was about, so how could she be so stupid? How could he be so stupid to trust the bitch?

CHAPTER 31

Dreek caught a glimpse of Monster's Range Rover pulling back up into the hood from his apartment window. He was watching a dice game that took place outside. He was contemplating if he wanted to go participate, or not when Monster rode pass. As he rode past, a thought jumped into his head. He grabbed his pistol and left the apartment.

He made it to Monster's apartment in no time since it was right across the street. He knocked on the door, and ZyAsia showed up in no time. "Hey, Dreek. Where you been?"

"Working hard, I really just got back in town a few days ago."

"Good for you. You here to see, Monster?" she asked while motioning for him to come in.

"You know I ain't here to see yo' big ass!" he spat jokingly.

She slapped him hard on the shoulder. "Monsterrrr! Come here."

"What? I got to help set up this party for tomorrow," he informed as he made his way into the living room.

"What party, what I miss?" Dreek asked as he came into view.

"Wassup, lil' nigga? Mazi just came back home."

Dreek took a seat on the arm of the lazy boy chair. "Toe-Tag's big brother?"

"Fuckin' right. My right-hand-man! He gave all that time back. Wassup, though, what you need?"

"When I was talking to you on the phone yesterday, you said something about Dead Shot being out of town right?"

"Yeah, why?"

Dreek shrugged his shoulders. "I ain't got the best vision around here, but I could've sworn I seen that nigga getting out a fancy-ass limo in Buckhead. Matter of fact, I know I saw that nigga. Ain't too many niggas got that head."

"You sure?" Monster took a seat on the couch, pulled his phone out, and dialed Dead Shot's number.

Dead Shot answered on the fourth ring, and Monster asked him where he was. He assured Monster that he was on the road, and everything was in line.

"Everything sounds good to me," said Monster after hanging up.

"I don't know, I'm sure I saw that nigga. Make sure you keep an eye on him. You can't ever forget where he came from."

"You right, you right."

Freddy was talking to, Vonte on video chat. He was still in the back of his BMW stretch limo. He was coming from a meeting with a realtor on a property he'd been having his eyes on for some time. Now he was just riding around the city wasting gas because he could.

"I just had a talk with that big head ass nigga, Dead Shot, like you said."

Vonte showed interest on his face. "Oh, yeah? What he say?"

"His loyalty is still with you."

"That fuck nigga only saying that because he knows I ain't dead yet."

Freddy nodded his head. "Basically, you know Toe-Tag's big brother just came home."

"Mazi, what that got to do with me?"

"Just thought you should know. He and Monster together was a helluva team back in their day. Now that Toe-Tag done grew up, all three of 'em gon' be a big problem."

"You don't even know the half. You'll see, though," Vonte stated smugly before ending the call.

172

New to the Game 2

Freddy hit the intercom, so he could communicate with his driver in the front. "Take me to my spot in Dunwoody."

***

Later that night, in Paradise East, Quay sat in the passenger's seat of Turk's cherry red E-Class Benz looking like the man in the middle of two huge stone boulders that were quickly closing in on him.

"So, let me get this right. That hoe, a muthafuckin' stripper, and she knew where *both* of your stashes was hidden?" Turk asked followed by heavy laughter. He couldn't believe Quay could be so stupid. He gave his partner more credit than that. Although he was laughing, he was definitely disappointed with the young nigga.

"I never thought she was gon' try no shit like that, honestly. She knows what I'm about, and what I do in these streets," Quay informed.

"A scorned woman will do *anything* to hurt whoever causing them pain. Come on, Quay. Now you sitting right here bringing this shit to me because you scared to tell them DG niggas," Turk barked.

"What would you do if one of your soldiers told you they did some shit like that?" asked Quay.

"His ass getting violated, and I'm gon' take his stripes until he whacks the hoe and go get that money back," Turk assured.

Quay pointed at him. "Exactly, I'm not trying to go through all that. I got to handle this *quietly*."

"You lucky I fuck with you because I really got too much going on to be going on secret missions, and shit."

Malik D. Rice

CHAPTER 32

Exotic Vibes was one of the hottest clubs in the city, and one of the newest. Rappers were mentioning the establishment in their songs, and all forms of celebrities were partying there regularly. It built a reputation for being a club for the *somebodies* of Atlanta. The admission fee was $100 in the regular line, and you didn't even want to talk about the VIP or the member's fees.

Mazi walked into the establishment with a glow in the dark VIP stamp on his hand. He and just about every Mobster from the hood. They were literally thirty deep in the spot.

Nobody but Toe-Tag was dressed appropriately, everybody else was looked like the definition of hoodlums.

"This shit niceeee! How long this muthafucka been open?" Mazi asked Toe-Tag as they walked into the large VIP area that was raised six feet above the crowd.

"About a year, and some change now."

The place looked so futuristic it was kind of hard to describe in words. Everything was so glossy and shiny. Mini stages appeared to be floating in thin air where exotic dancers danced half-naked. There were bars, couches, chill-stations, and separate dance floors all throughout the place. It almost looked better than Gilmore's lobby.

"This shit like a strip club, and a lounge, all in one," Mazi concluded while looking around with the amazement of a little kid.

Toe-Tag wasn't as impressed. Papa held the Dons meeting at the club about two months ago, so he knew what to expect. "That ain't shit. You been looking around so much, you forgot to look down."

Mazi's head shot down to his feet, and his eyes almost popped out of his head. "Man, I know them ain't no baby sharks in the floor?"

"Hell yeah, these folks went overboard."

They proceeded to enjoying themselves and turning up for Mazi's freedom. Everybody enjoyed themselves, but Toe-Tag just sat back and watched them have fun. He had too much on his mind. He was thinking of a plan for Mazi. He didn't want to lose his big brother to the system again, or worse, but he knew how Mazi was. There wasn't a soul that could keep him out of the game.

***

LaKisha was a hardworking woman trying to raise a man on her own. She was raised in the hood but never allowed herself to be a hood rat. She tried to raise Quavo in the same fashion her mother raised her, but it wasn't that easy. Unfortunately, she'd fallen into the single-mother category with a deadbeat baby's father. So, Quavo had to look around for father-figures in his life, and all the father-figures around her way were the wrong figures.

When she came home from work and saw Quavo sitting on the couch counting a sizable bankroll with a fresh DG tattoo on his neck, she stopped in her tracks and just stood there with tears falling down her cheeks.

Quavo looked up and saw her crying. He tried to give her some money, and assured her that he would be alright, and not to worry about him. She turned the money down, stared at him in disgust, and went to her room.

That was about a week ago, and she hadn't spoken to him since. She didn't lecture him because there was no point, and she didn't kick him out because she didn't have the heart to do it. She just let him be and prayed harder than she ever had in her life. She prayed for God to protect her only son.

It was 1:00 a.m., and Quavo still hadn't come home. She was laying down with her eyes closed praying that God kept an eye on her baby boy, when she heard the front door open, and shut. She had a *strong* urge to jump up out of the bed, rush to the door, and wrap him in her arms, but she had to remember that she was supposed to be mad at him. She decided on staying in the bed but was *very* relieved that he had made it home. She didn't know how long she could put up with this.

Instead of going straight to his room, as usual, Quavo, opened her door and walked in the room dressed in all black. It was only then that she popped up.

"Quavo?" She could see him clearly through the streetlight that shined through the window.

He didn't answer her. He just stood there for a few long seconds staring at her before walking over to her bed and climbing in it with her. He got up under the covers and curled up like he used to when he was little. He hadn't laid in her bed in over five years.

She got closer to him where she could see his face and saw the tears rolling down his face. He laid there with his eyes open looking at her, but he wasn't actually looking at her. It was like he was looking through her. The boy that slept in her bed wasn't her son, he was somebody else.

"Baby, what's wrong!" she asked desperately, but he wouldn't talk. He just laid there staring blankly with tears coming out of his eyes.

She could hear his heavy breathing. It was tearing her up inside. She didn't know it was going to happen this fast, but this is exactly the reality she'd been trying to protect him from, but how could she stop it when he was running towards it? Either he'd witness a murder or participated in one. She was hoping at least it was the first, but by the look in his eyes, she feared that it was the latter.

She scooted closer to him and pulled him in for an embrace. It was then that he let it out. He started sobbing. He held her tight and sobbed for a whole twenty minutes before eventually drifting off to sleep in her arms.

Long after he fell asleep, she laid awake with her mind in overdrive. She was going to make Toe-Tag, and Monster, pay for taking her son's soul.

CHAPTER 33

Pooh Bear was a notorious stick-up kid on the Southside. He was an OG for the Neighborhood Rolling 60 Crips in the Old National boulevard area, and he was also Diamond's big brother.

"I did my homework on that, nigga," Turk informed. "You can't get nobody around here to say nothing bad about him unless he done robbed them, and some of them niggas won't even say nothing bad about the nigga."

Quay waved him off. "Man, I don't want to hear all that shit. He can get whacked just like any other nigga."

It was 3:26 a.m., and they were sitting in Quay's old Audi scoping out Diamond and Pooh Bear's mother's house. She stayed in a middle-class neighborhood about twenty minutes off Old National boulevard with her husband and their ten-year-old son.

"This bitch gon' cross a nigga like me knowing she got unattended family out here."

He knew Diamond's real name, so it wasn't hard to look her up then find her mother. The internet was a muthafucka.

"We been out here for a while, and ain't nobody come in or out this bitch. It's two cars in the driveway, and the lights on, so somebody got to be in there."

Turk looked at him very seriously. "Look, the *only* reason I'm really out here with you is because I didn't want your stupid ass coming out here by yourself, but I'm gon' let you know this here. If this shit blows up in our face, I was never here."

"Just chill, I ain't gon' do nothing stupid tonight. We gon' snatch the lil' boy up tomorrow at the park."

"How the hell you know he gon' be at the park?"

"Because Diamond stupid ass in love with that lil' boy, she always talking about him. He go to the park *every day*."

***

"I don't know the first thing about the production business. You want me to invest in some shit that I don't know nothing about?" Papa said. He was in Toe-Tag's condo sitting the living room.

"I want you to invest in some shit that's gon' quadruple your money, and some," Toe-Tag assured. He wasn't sitting down like Papa he paced the floor with his hands behind his back.

"A movie is one thing, but you trying to film a TV series and post it on YouTube. The last time I checked YouTube was free."

"After you get a certain amount of views, they offer you a deal where you get paid off your views."

Papa smirked up at him, he was very proud that Toe-Tag was trying to elevate, and do something better than wreck-havoc, which is why he agreed to invest in the positive cause, but at the same time, he had to protect his money. He wasn't trying to take any losses.

"Okay, I'll invest the five-hundred gees under *one* condition."

Toe-Tag stopped pacing and look down at him with hopeful eyes. "What?"

"Sale the series on DVDs. Make them an hour-long, and charge five-dollars a-piece or some shit."

"Deal." They shook hands and sealed the deal.

Dreek and Mooski were at the shooting range with their kill team's critiquing their skills. Freddy had property in the Tucker, Georgia and turned a vacant building into a shooting range that Dilluminati could use privately. Monster made it mandatory that *everyone* in their camp learns how to shoot correctly. That situation with Mooski inspired the idea.

Mooski held a fully equipped AR-15 with one hand while watching Dreek shoot at his target with an MP5. "I don't know how you caught all them bodies you got with that ugly ass shooting you be doing."

Dreek didn't entertain him, he just continued shooting. Trying his hardest to focus, but Mooski hated to be ignored, and wouldn't let up.

"You started fucking with that thot ass bitch, Mesha, from Second Ave? You got that hoe all on yo' page. What the hell wrong with you?"

As soon as Dreek's clip was empty, he spun on Mooski. "Lil' nigga, don't be worrying about who I'm fucking. I don't even fuck with you like that. Just because we in the same camp don't mean we got to converse."

Mooski screwed his face up. "Nigga, fuck you! I was just trying to be nice to yo' lame-ass. I don't know what got into you, but you been acting like a real *bitch* lately."

"This coming from the same nigga who was crying in front of his bitch! Soft-ass-nigga! What, can't take the heat? The bodies catching up to you?"

By now he was all up in Mooski's face, and the tension in the room was growing thicker and thicker. Both kill-teams were drawing near their superiors ready for a civil war if it came down to it, and it did.

Mooski caught Dreek with an uppercut that made his mouth close causing his teeth to clang together painfully. He followed up with a series of combinations. Before they knew it, a full brawl had erupted. You could hear guns dropping on the smooth granite floor, grunts, and insults, as they went at it.

The funny part was that everybody lived in the same hood, and they were going at it like they didn't even know each other, but only two people would have to answer to the Don.

CHAPTER 34

Shanay was at Phat's house helping her cook food for the family dinner that they were throwing.

Toe-Tag was still at their condo handling a little business. He was sitting on his couch listening to Dreek and Mooski explain themselves. Mazi and Monster stood silently on either side of them, towering over them like small buildings.

"Wait!" Toe-Tag interrupted with a hand in the air. "Ain't none of y'all right. Both of y'all in the wrong and got to pay the consequences. Y'all setting a bad example for the Mobsters. Fucking up the structure of our camp. If I let this go then niggas gon' think it's okay. So, both of y'all niggas got to pay a four-thousand-dollar fee every week for four weeks." Dreek sucked his teeth. "Problem?" Toe-Tag asked sternly.

Dreek shook his head with an unpleasant look on his face. He didn't have anything nice to say, so he opted the smart way, and didn't say anything at all.

"Get out my spot man. Y'all two niggas on thin ice. If I hear something else out y'all niggas, it's not gon' be pretty," he promised.

They both turned to leave, but Mazi grabbed Mooski's arm yanking him backward.

"What the fuck wrong with you?" he asked Mazi heatedly with his chest poked out. He was already mad about the damn fee, now this nigga was roughing him up. He was about ready to uppercut his big ass.

"I need to talk to you," Toe-Tag informed matter-of-factly.

"What's up, big bro'?"

"That fight wasn't the only thing I heard about today."

Last night, Mooski had caught Babie in the park kicking it with some of the Dinero, and PDE, girls she fucked with. He was so mad at the fact that she had told his business that he slapped her to the ground in front of everybody, and basically dragged her back to their apartment where he beat her some more.

It wasn't until then, that Mooski considered the fact that Babie was the sister of Toe-Tag's best friend. "I was just mad she told my business like tho, man. I ain't even hit her that hard."

Mazi caught him with his famous left-handed hook and knocked him out cold. All three of them looked down at Mooski sprawled out the floor awkwardly.

"God damn, bro'! I said rough him up, not kill the nigga."

Mazi laughed his usual demonic laugh. "He ain't dead—I ain't even hit him that hard!" he joked spitefully.

Meanwhile, on the other side of town. Quay sat in an abandoned house right off Jonesboro Road, around the corner from where his aunt stayed. It wasn't a nasty house. A family had just moved out of it a few months ago, and there was a for sale sign in the front. So, Quay broke in so he could use it as a holding place for Diamond's little brother, Lil' Mann.

Turk had deserted him after he helped him snatch up Lil' Mann. He did his part and got far away from the situation. He knew Quay was going about it the wrong way, but he couldn't tell Quay anything, so he just left him alone.

The water was running in the house, but the electricity was off. He sat in the living room on the floor staring around the empty dark room. His thoughts were going a million miles per hour. He was trying to figure out his next move.

His phone vibrated on the floor, and it startled him making him jump a little. He picked it up and looked at the screen. It was one of his baby mothers. He swiped the phone to ignore the call and put placed the phone back on the ground.

Lil' Mann was tied up in one of the bedrooms in the back, and he had to make a move because he wouldn't be able to

184

keep shit quiet for too much longer. Diamond would start causing a scene, and his cover would be blown soon after that.

He looked down at Lil' Mann's phone and picked it up. He turned it on and put the password in that he made Lil' Mann give to him. The lil' nigga had 263 missed calls, and he'd only been missing got eight hours.

Quay found Diamond's number and dialed it. She answered on the second ring. "Hello! Lil' Mann?" she answered urgently with heavy concern in her voice.

"Why you sound so worried? Your brother in good hands."

She gasped audibly. "Quay! You better not touch my muthafuckin' brother!"

"Touch him, why would I do that? It's not like I'm a killer or nothing. I'm just a lil' bitch ass nigga. That's why you took my money, right?" he said sarcastically.

"Listen, Quay, I was going to give you your shit back. I just was trying to get you back for hurting me."

Quay smiled because he could hear the weakness in her voice and could tell that she'd been crying. He had her right where he wanted her. "Fuck all that! Go to my spot and put *everything* back exactly where you got it from. Then put my apartment key on the coffee table and get the fuck on. After I count all my money to make sure it's all there, I'll give you an address to pick the lil' fuck nigga up at."

Malik D. Rice

CHAPTER 35

Mooski woke up in his bed feeling like warm dog shit. Mazi caught him on the temple. That whole area of his head and face was throbbing and swollen. He was really lucky that his jaw wasn't wired shut, but of course, he didn't perceive things that way. He felt betrayed by Toe-Tag. He kicked all that brother loyalty shit, then turn around and handle him like a stranger on the street. He was wrong for putting his hands on Babie, but he didn't think Toe-Tag was supposed to let shit go down like that.

Babie walked in the room barely dressed. "You alright, baby?" she asked when she saw him sitting up. "It's about time you woke your ass up. You wasn't even supposed to go to sleep, but you so damn hardheaded."

"Fuck a concussion, go bring me some pain pills, man. My head hurt like hell. If that fuck nigga Mazi was another nigga his ass would've got whacked."

"That's how yo' ass got in this predicament in the first place. You can't run around here doing reckless shit thinking that it ain't gon' be no consequences."

His face twisted up into his famous mug. "Fuck you using all them big words for?"

"Boyyy!" She slapped her forehead out of frustration. "You a damn mess! I love you, though. I was wrong for telling your business. I knew you was just mad, and you love me, too. I forgive you for it, and that's all that matters. Just don't be mad at Toe-Tag, though. He had to show you a lil' discipline. If he let you get away with everything you gon' think you can do anything."

She turned around and left to go get him some pain pills, and he laid there reflecting real hard on the jewels she had just dropped on him. Rampage had taught her well. She was a good girl for a nigga like him to have on his side.

***

Kapo sat behind his desk in his office looking at Sheriff McFarland once again.

"You've cleaned the streets of DeKalb county up, and I'm very pleased."

Kapo smiled faintly. "I wouldn't have it any other way, and I'm pleased with the help I've been receiving on your end as far as the Intel goes."

"No problem. No problem at all." He looked over at the brown paper bag that sat on Kapo's desk expectantly.

"Oh, this is for you," said Kapo catching on to the gesture. "Just another little contribution for the *community*."

McFarland peeked inside the bag, and a wave of pleasure came washing over him. "We thank you very much. Everything's smooth with Dilluminati in DeKalb county, but you might want to talk to your guys over in Clayton county, the FBI just set their sights on them."

"Thank you for the tip, Sheriff. Enjoy the rest of your day, I'll be in contact."

McFarland got up and left the office room. Kapo remained behind his desk gathering his thoughts. He'd been spending way more time in his office than he has at any of his homes. Life has consisted of work for him lately, he wasn't making any time for personal. He was still secretly grieving the losses of his wife, and daughter. They were his rock, so now all he had was Dilluminati.

Before he knew it, he had fallen asleep laid back in his chair. Fifty minutes later, he was awakened by Glock's hand on his shoulder. He woke up startled, and discombobulated. "What?"

"Ms. Sung is here for her five 'o'clock appointment."

Kapo sighed heavily while running both hands down his face. "Let her in."

"You got it, Boss."

Ms. Sung walked in looking marvelous in a peach-colored sundress that flared out at the bottom, and pretty, white, open-toe sandals that showed her pretty feet. All that was cool, but it was the way she wore her long, silky hair straight down that caused the erection in his pants.

He stood up, walked around the desk, and embraced her. "You look great, Mina," he said before kissing her on her thin lips.

"Thank you, Hunny. You don't look too bad yourself. Can we talk?"

He looked down at her expectantly. "I was thinking we could relieve a little stress before we got into all of that."

His hands was now up under her skirt caressing her little booty loving the feel of her smooth skin, and the smoothness from the fabric of the panties she wore. By now, his dick was harder than a convict.

"No, babe, we need to talk now. This is serious," she said while pushing him off her because if he kept touching, she'd definitely fall victim to his seduction. Her pussy was already a little moist just by his touch.

He walked over to the couch and took a seat. The couch had good size on it, but she chose to take a seat in his lap.

She put an arm around his neck for support. "You've been a busy man lately, but you still make time for me, and I appreciate that."

"You breaking up with me?" he joked seriously.

"I didn't know we were in a relationship?"

He looked up at her through squinted eyes. "You know my situation. What we got is the closest thing to a relationship I got outside of business."

"Good, because I'm pregnant, Kareem. And I'm very aware of your situation. So, I came here to see if you wanted to keep it or get rid of it."

CHAPTER 36

It was Wednesday night at club Ritz on Old National Boulevard. The Ritz was a place where you could go party and have you a good time. AK was due to perform tonight, and a lot of people showed up to see the rising star.

He was quickly making the transition from a C-list artist into a B-list artist, with DG Records behind him, he was sure to continue succeeding. He sat in the back of a rented Escalade that was parked in the VIP area in front of the club looking out the window at the long line of people. Everyone was there to see him, and it was a good feeling. He could hear his songs bumping from the stereo systems in people's cars in the parking lot.

"There she go right there," his right-hand-man, and road manager, Mayday informed.

The club promoter was walking towards them with the mandatory $15,000 that AK charged for each show. She was an attractive plus-size woman in her mid-thirties. They got out of the truck to greet her.

"Here you go. All blue strips like you requested," she said while handing Mayday a manila envelope with a little width to it.

Mayday tried to accept the envelope out of her hand, but she wouldn't let go. "Aren't you forgetting something?" She had her phone in her other hand extended towards him.

He smiled showing his small white teeth, grabbed her phone, and saved his name in it before giving it back. She called the number to make sure it was his real number. It wasn't until then that she released the envelope and walked back to the club.

Mayday looked around at his peers who were staring at him amusingly. "What?"

"You into big girls now?" asked AK.

"I'm into *that* big girl right there."

They proceeded across the parking lot on their way into the club when a small group of masked men hopped out of one of the cars in the parking lot with automatic rifles and started blasting towards them.

AK never made it to the stage.

***

It was an ordinary Thursday afternoon when Dead Shot pulled up into Sun Valley with three Mobsters from his kill-team. He wasn't being summoned, but he still pulled up.

Monster wasn't at his spot, and he wasn't answering the phone, so he called, Toe-Tag who was holed up in his condo as usual. Toe-Tag invited him up, so he left his kill-team who was lounging around the Yukon and walked to Toe-Tag's spot.

Mazi opened the door with an MP-5 in hand. "Wassup?" He moved out the way so Dead Shot could walkthrough.

Toe-Tag was on the couch smoking a blunt of weed watching a thriller movie on Netflix.

"You want me to stand up?" Dead Shot asked awkwardly because he didn't want to just sit down and disrespect the Don.

"Man, sit yo' ass down. I did invite you in here. Plus, I'm not power struck. Wassup, though?"

Dead Shot took a seat. "Nothing, much, just really checking in. I rarely get summoned by you, but I haven't been hearing from Monster lately. Usually, he'll keep something for a nigga to do, or something. He been distant lately."

"Oh, yeah?" Toe-Tag asked faking ignorance. He knew all about the rumors of Dead Shot meeting up with Freddy secretly. "Why you think he acting like that, though?"

"I don't know, he probably got something going on. Niggas like us go through shit all the time."

"Yeah, trust issues."

Dead Shot tried hard to conceal the alertness he felt by the comment. "What makes you say that?"

Toe-Tag laughed silently with a smug expression on his face. "What separates one side of the field from the other?"

"Uhhh, a line."

"Exactly! That line can be thick for some niggas, and thin as paper for others."

"What you getting at?"

"Just a lil' something for you to think about on your ride back home."

Dead Shot caught on to the dismissive response, so he stood up. "My loyalty lies with y'all, Loyalty 4 Eva."

Dreek was sitting on the stairs of the building across from Toe-Tag's watching as Dead Shot get back in the back of the Yukon with disgust. He wanted to end the nigga right there, but he had way more sense than that. He knew what he saw downtown that day though. He knew Dead Shot wasn't right.

He put the orange Crush soda bottle up to his mouth and drained the last few swallows before tossing it onto the ground a few feet away from him.

"That's why the hood so damn dirty. Black ass niggas like you always littering," a young voice joked from behind.

He quickly stood up on the stairs and looked over the rail down at, Quavo who was smirking up at him evilly. "Lil' nigga, what the hell I tell you about sneaking up on me like that?" he spat sternly.

All the Young Mobsters who weren't on kill-teams were assigned to Mafiosos that they'd answer to and take orders from. Sort of like they had their own camp inside of Toe-Tag's.

Quavo was assigned to Dreek's camp and has been a pain in his ass ever since.

"You heard about AK getting shot at that club on the Southside?" he asked while making his way up the stairs.

"Yeah, they did, my nigga dirty."

"What we gon' do about it?"

"It's Wopp's call because he over the Southside, but if he needs our help, we gon' slide out there, and tear that shit up."

Quavo used both hands to take out the braids he had in his head while looking at Dreek knowingly.

"No, you can't come."

"You lame as hell, man." Although Quavo played disappointed, he was really relieved deep down inside.

The last mission that he went on and the shit that he witnessed had him scarred for life. That experience made him reconsider his goals of being on anybody's kill-team. He didn't have a problem putting in work, robbing niggas, or participating in a heist, but he didn't want any parts of the murder game. All that being said, he was scared to let it be known, so he had to fake his thirst for blood.

"Just enjoy your childhood, and your soul, while you still got it, lil' nigga."

CHAPTER 37

Turk was standing in front of the Texaco on Bouldercrest Road posted up with his soldiers while they served the crack fiends, and weed heads, in the vicinity. It was a nice, and hot summer day so he figured he'd kick it on the block with them for the day.

Quay's Audi pulled up into the gas station. He hopped out looking like a bag of money with all his jewelry on, and big lumps in the pockets of his skinny jeans.

"See you done found your fortune," said Turk as Quay neared.

"Fuck you. Let me chop it up with you real quick," he requested while looking around at all the shooters that were clinging onto him like the president.

Turk told his soldiers to give him some privacy so they could have a made-man conversation. "Wassup, lil' bruh?"

"Mannn, I know you heard about that shit with AK?"

"Who ain't heard about it?"

Quay leaned a little closer with a stone-like expression on his face. "I got a bad feeling this shit gon' blow up in my face. When niggas start having sit-downs, and they ask the reason behind that shit, my ass gon' be grass, shawty."

"You think Pooh Bear had something to do with that?"

"Come on, man. You did your homework on the nigga just like me. You know don't nothing happen without his approval, and the fact that it happened after I snatched his lil' brother up makes a lot of sense. It would've been more understanding if they would've run down on, AK, and robbed him, but they just pulled up spraying without taking nothing. Wopp, and Toe-Tag, gon' definitely want answers. Shit, Dinero himself gon' want answers because AK was starting to make DG Records a lot of money. I'm dead, shawty!"

Turk could see the fear in his young nigga's eyes. It was a mystery how someone who took lives for a living could be scared to die themselves. If it was somebody else, he probably would've told them to suck it up, and that it comes with the game, but he looked at Quay like the little brother he never had. He couldn't just sit there and watch his downfall.

"You good, lil' bruh. You know how I'm rocking. If it comes down to it, I'll just take you up under my wing and stamp you PDE. If DG want smoke, then it is what it is, but I ain't gon' let nothing happen to you."

Quay shook his head disapprovingly. "Nah, I won't be the cause of that. I'll figure it out."

"I don't know why you tripping. You got your money back and can't nobody prove you did shit. Only person that could tell on you is yourself because you know I won't tell. If I tell on you, I'll be telling on my damn self. The shit ain't never happen!"

Quay nodded with a little hope in his eyes, and a growing smile on his acne-filled face. "What was we talking about again?"

"This new strip club in Cobb county. I hear they had some hoes imported from overseas to dance at that muthafucka."

"Worddd? We got to go check that out."

"Facts."

They would never speak on the situation again. It was going to the grave.

***

"So, you're telling us that you're willing to jump into that lifestyle and report back to us on the regular?" asked Agent Chinx while sitting across from a potential informant in an interrogation room.

"Yes."

"According to your file, it says that you've been staying in the hood your whole life? I'm sure crime has been going on in that hood forever. Why wait until now to try and bring them down? It has to be some kind of motivation behind this decision."

"I have my reasons. Just know that I'm going to go deep undercover to bring them down. Whatever information you need to put them away, I'll get it for you."

Chinx looked at him suspiciously. "Please state your full name, so I can print out a contract. You'll get paid for your services, and there are certain benefits to working with the FBI that will be printed in the contract."

"I'll have to have a lawyer go over that."

"Fine by me. Name?"

She took a deep breath and closed her eyes as she exhaled. "Lakisha Grant."

To Be Continued...
New to the Game 3
Coming Soon

Malik D. Rice

Submission Guideline

Submit the first three chapters of your completed manuscript to ldpsubmissions@gmail.com, subject line: Your book's title. The manuscript must be in a .doc file and sent as an attachment. Document should be in Times New Roman, double spaced and in size 12 font. Also, provide your synopsis and full contact information. If sending multiple submissions, they must each be in a separate email.

Have a story but no way to send it electronically? You can still submit to LDP/Ca$h Presents. Send in the first three chapters, written or typed, of your completed manuscript to:

LDP: Submissions Dept
Po Box 944
Stockbridge, Ga 30281

DO NOT send original manuscript. Must be a duplicate.

Provide your synopsis and a cover letter containing your full contact information.

Thanks for considering LDP and Ca$h Presents.

New to the Game 2

Coming Soon from Lock Down Publications/Ca$h Presents

BOW DOWN TO MY GANGSTA

By **Ca$h**

TORN BETWEEN TWO

By **Coffee**

THE STREETS STAINED MY SOUL **II**

By **Marcellus Allen**

BLOOD OF A BOSS **VI**

SHADOWS OF THE GAME II

By **Askari**

LOYAL TO THE GAME **IV**

By **T.J. & Jelissa**

A DOPEBOY'S PRAYER **II**

By **Eddie "Wolf" Lee**

IF LOVING YOU IS WRONG... **III**

By **Jelissa**

TRUE SAVAGE **VII**

MIDNIGHT CARTEL III

DOPE BOY MAGIC III

By **Chris Green**

BLAST FOR ME **III**

A SAVAGE DOPEBOY III

CUTTHROAT MAFIA II

By **Ghost**

A HUSTLER'S DECEIT III

KILL ZONE **II**

Malik D. Rice

BAE BELONGS TO ME III
By **Aryanna**
CHAINED TO THE STREETS III
By **J-Blunt**
KING OF NEW YORK V
COKE KINGS IV
BORN HEARTLESS IV
By **T.J. Edwards**
GORILLAZ IN THE BAY V
TEARS OF A GANGSTA II
De'Kari
THE STREETS ARE CALLING II
Duquie Wilson
KINGPIN KILLAZ IV
STREET KINGS III
PAID IN BLOOD III
CARTEL KILLAZ IV
DOPE GODS II
Hood Rich
SINS OF A HUSTLA II
ASAD
TRIGGADALE III
Elijah R. Freeman
KINGZ OF THE GAME V
Playa Ray
SLAUGHTER GANG IV
RUTHLESS HEART IV

By Willie Slaughter

THE HEART OF A SAVAGE III

By Jibril Williams

FUK SHYT II

By Blakk Diamond

THE DOPEMAN'S BODYGAURD II

By Tranay Adams

TRAP GOD II

By Troublesome

YAYO III

A SHOOTER'S AMBITION III

By S. Allen

GHOST MOB

Stilloan Robinson

KINGPIN DREAMS II

By Paper Boi Rari

CREAM

By Yolanda Moore

SON OF A DOPE FIEND II

By Renta

FOREVER GANGSTA II

GLOCKS ON SATIN SHEETS II

By Adrian Dulan

LOYALTY AIN'T PROMISED II

By Keith Williams

THE PRICE YOU PAY FOR LOVE II

DOPE GIRL MAGIC II

Malik D. Rice

By Destiny Skai
THE LIFE OF A HOOD STAR
By Rashia Wilson
TOE TAGZ III
By Ah'Million
CONFESSIONS OF A GANGSTA II
By Nicholas Lock
PAID IN KARMA III
By **Meesha**
I'M NOTHING WITHOUT HIS LOVE II
By Monet Dragun
CAUGHT UP IN THE LIFE II
By Robert Baptiste
NEW TO THE GAME III
By **Malik D. Rice**
Life of a Savage III
By **Romell Tukes**
Quiet Money II
By **Trai'Quan**
THE STREETS MADE ME II
By **Larry D. Wright**
THE ULTIMATE SACRIFICE VI
By **Anthony Fields**

<u>Available Now</u>

RESTRAINING ORDER **I & II**

By **CA$H & Coffee**

LOVE KNOWS NO BOUNDARIES **I II & III**

By **Coffee**

RAISED AS A GOON I, II, III & IV

BRED BY THE SLUMS I, II, III

BLAST FOR ME I & II

ROTTEN TO THE CORE I II III

A BRONX TALE I, II, III

DUFFEL BAG CARTEL I II III IV

HEARTLESS GOON I II III IV

A SAVAGE DOPEBOY I II

HEARTLESS GOON I II III

DRUG LORDS I II III

CUTTHROAT MAFIA

By **Ghost**

LAY IT DOWN **I & II**

LAST OF A DYING BREED

BLOOD STAINS OF A SHOTTA I & II III

By **Jamaica**

LOYAL TO THE GAME I II III

LIFE OF SIN I, II III

By **TJ & Jelissa**

BLOODY COMMAS I & II

SKI MASK CARTEL I II & III

KING OF NEW YORK I II,III IV

RISE TO POWER I II III

COKE KINGS I II III

BORN HEARTLESS I II III

By **T.J. Edwards**

IF LOVING HIM IS WRONG…I & II

LOVE ME EVEN WHEN IT HURTS I II III

By **Jelissa**

WHEN THE STREETS CLAP BACK I & II III

THE HEART OF A SAVAGE I II

By **Jibril Williams**

A DISTINGUISHED THUG STOLE MY HEART I II & III

LOVE SHOULDN'T HURT I II III IV

RENEGADE BOYS I II III IV

PAID IN KARMA I II

By **Meesha**

A GANGSTER'S CODE I &, II III

A GANGSTER'S SYN I II III

THE SAVAGE LIFE I II III

CHAINED TO THE STREETS I II

By J-Blunt

PUSH IT TO THE LIMIT

By **Bre' Hayes**

BLOOD OF A BOSS **I, II, III, IV, V**

SHADOWS OF THE GAME

By **Askari**

THE STREETS BLEED MURDER **I, II & III**

THE HEART OF A GANGSTA I II& III

By **Jerry Jackson**

CUM FOR ME I II III IV V

An **LDP Erotica Collaboration**

BRIDE OF A HUSTLA **I II & II**

THE FETTI GIRLS **I, II& III**

CORRUPTED BY A GANGSTA I, II III, IV

BLINDED BY HIS LOVE

THE PRICE YOU PAY FOR LOVE

DOPE GIRL MAGIC

By **Destiny Skai**

WHEN A GOOD GIRL GOES BAD

By **Adrienne**

THE COST OF LOYALTY I II III

By Kweli

A GANGSTER'S REVENGE **I II III & IV**

THE BOSS MAN'S DAUGHTERS I II III IV V

A SAVAGE LOVE **I & II**

BAE BELONGS TO ME I II

A HUSTLER'S DECEIT I, II, III

WHAT BAD BITCHES DO I, II, III

SOUL OF A MONSTER I II III

KILL ZONE

By **Aryanna**

A KINGPIN'S AMBITON

A KINGPIN'S AMBITION **II**

I MURDER FOR THE DOUGH

Malik D. Rice

By **Ambitious**
TRUE SAVAGE I II III IV V VI
DOPE BOY MAGIC I, II
MIDNIGHT CARTEL I II
By **Chris Green**
A DOPEBOY'S PRAYER
By **Eddie "Wolf" Lee**
THE KING CARTEL **I, II & III**
By **Frank Gresham**
THESE NIGGAS AIN'T LOYAL **I, II & III**
By **Nikki Tee**
GANGSTA SHYT **I II &III**
By **CATO**
THE ULTIMATE BETRAYAL
By **Phoenix**
BOSS'N UP **I , II & III**
By **Royal Nicole**
I LOVE YOU TO DEATH
By Destiny J
I RIDE FOR MY HITTA
I STILL RIDE FOR MY HITTA
By **Misty Holt**
LOVE & CHASIN' PAPER
By **Qay Crockett**
TO DIE IN VAIN
SINS OF A HUSTLA
By **ASAD**

206

BROOKLYN HUSTLAZ

By **Boogsy Morina**

BROOKLYN ON LOCK I & II

By **Sonovia**

GANGSTA CITY

By **Teddy Duke**

A DRUG KING AND HIS DIAMOND I & II III

A DOPEMAN'S RICHES

HER MAN, MINE'S TOO I, II

CASH MONEY HO'S

By Nicole Goosby

TRAPHOUSE KING **I II & III**

KINGPIN KILLAZ I II III

STREET KINGS I II

PAID IN BLOOD **I II**

CARTEL KILLAZ I II III

DOPE GODS

By **Hood Rich**

LIPSTICK KILLAH **I, II, III**

CRIME OF PASSION I II & III

By **Mimi**

STEADY MOBBN' **I, II, III**

THE STREETS STAINED MY SOUL

By **Marcellus Allen**

WHO SHOT YA **I, II, III**

SON OF A DOPE FIEND

Renta

Malik D. Rice

GORILLAZ IN THE BAY **I II III IV**

TEARS OF A GANGSTA

DE'KARI

TRIGGADALE I II

Elijah R. Freeman

GOD BLESS THE TRAPPERS I, II, III

THESE SCANDALOUS STREETS I, II, III

FEAR MY GANGSTA I, II, III

THESE STREETS DON'T LOVE NOBODY I, II

BURY ME A G I, II, III, IV, V

A GANGSTA'S EMPIRE I, II, III, IV

THE DOPEMAN'S BODYGAURD

Tranay Adams

THE STREETS ARE CALLING

Duquie Wilson

MARRIED TO A BOSS... I II III

By Destiny Skai & Chris Green

KINGZ OF THE GAME I II III IV

Playa Ray

SLAUGHTER GANG I II III

RUTHLESS HEART I II III

By Willie Slaughter

FUK SHYT

By Blakk Diamond

DON'T F#CK WITH MY HEART I II

By Linnea

ADDICTED TO THE DRAMA I II III

By Jamila

YAYO I II

A SHOOTER'S AMBITION I II

By S. Allen

TRAP GOD

By Troublesome

FOREVER GANGSTA

GLOCKS ON SATIN SHEETS

By Adrian Dulan

TOE TAGZ I II

By Ah'Million

KINGPIN DREAMS

By Paper Boi Rari

CONFESSIONS OF A GANGSTA

By Nicholas Lock

I'M NOTHING WITHOUT HIS LOVE

By Monet Dragun

CAUGHT UP IN THE LIFE

By Robert Baptiste

NEW TO THE GAME I II

By **Malik D. Rice**

Life of a Savage I II

By **Romell Tukes**

LOYALTY AIN'T PROMISED

By Keith Williams

Quiet Money

By **Trai'Quan**

Malik D. Rice

THE STREETS MADE ME
By **Larry D. Wright**
THE ULTIMATE SACRIFICE I, II, III, IV, V
By **Anthony Fields**

BOOKS BY LDP'S CEO, CA$H

TRUST IN NO MAN

TRUST IN NO MAN 2

TRUST IN NO MAN 3

BONDED BY BLOOD

SHORTY GOT A THUG

THUGS CRY

THUGS CRY 2

THUGS CRY 3

TRUST NO BITCH

TRUST NO BITCH 2

TRUST NO BITCH 3

TIL MY CASKET DROPS

RESTRAINING ORDER

RESTRAINING ORDER 2

IN LOVE WITH A CONVICT

Coming Soon

BONDED BY BLOOD 2

BOW DOWN TO MY GANGSTA

Malik D. Rice